D1564090

"So the loser will shoot the victor," Carter taunted.

Rudzutak held the P6 with both hands, shaking, ready to kill Carter, a wicked grin spreading over his granitelike face . . .

The bark of the gun was loud. The front of Rudzutak's skull mushroomed forward, blowing away flesh, bone, and blood to splatter the ground around him.

Odah emerged in all her naked womanhood, holding Carter's cherished 9mm Luger still smoking in her left hand.

"I had him in my sights all the time," she said, "but you were doing too well."

She looked at him through eyes wet with passion and excitement . . .

NICK CARTER IS IT!

"Nick Carter out-Bonds James Bond."
                            —*Buffalo Evening News*

"Nick Carter is America's #1 espionage agent."
                            —*Variety*

"Nick Carter is razor-sharp suspense."
                            —*King Features*

"Nick Carter has attracted an army of addicted readers . . . the books are fast, have plenty of action and just the right degree of sex . . . Nick Carter is the American James Bond, suave, sophisticated, a killer with both the ladies and the enemy."
                            —*The New York Times*

FROM THE NICK CARTER
KILLMASTER SERIES

AFGHAN INTERCEPT

KILL
MASTER
NICK CARTER

JOVE BOOKS, NEW YORK

"Nick Carter" is a registered trademark of The Condé Nast
Publications, Inc., registered in the United States Patent Office.

KILLMASTER #242: AFGHAN INTERCEPT

A Jove Book / published by arrangement with
The Condé Nast Publications, Inc.

PRINTING HISTORY
Jove edition / October 1988

All rights reserved.
Copyright © 1988 by The Condé Nast Publications, Inc.
This book may not be reproduced in whole or in part,
by mimeograph or any other means, without permission.
For information address: The Berkley Publishing Group,
200 Madison Avenue, New York, New York 10016.

ISBN: 0-515-09757-8

Jove Books are published by The Berkley Publishing Group,
200 Madison Avenue, New York, New York 10016.
The name "JOVE" and the "J" logo
are trademarks belonging to Jove Publications, Inc.

PRINTED IN THE UNITED STATES OF AMERICA

10 9 8 7 6 5 4 3 2 1

*Dedicated to the men of the
Secret Services of the
United States of America*

ONE

The wind blew white powder along the broad asphalt surface of Zubovskiy Boulevard, the snow sometimes whirling and dancing in small tornadolike tubes, ballerinas toeing their way across a stage. The few Muscovites out that night walked with their heads into the wind, the fine white flakes finding their way between the folds of their clothing and beneath fur hats, chilling skin already tortured by a long and bitter winter.

One man stood alone in a doorway watching the windows and entrance of the apartment building on the other side of the wide thoroughfare. He was dressed in a poorly tailored suit of rough wool, the product of a faltering economy. His greatcoat was cut long, in the military fashion. It was black to match his suit. He wore an old fur hat with earflaps hanging loose, blowing in the wind. He was a big man, more than six feet tall, and in the bulky clothes, he weighed in at well over two hundred pounds.

The man looked older than his years, his skin pulled tight and shining in the subzero temperature. The skin was a plastic mask covering makeup filler used to broaden the face, heighten the bone structure of the eyebrows and chin. The disguise was perfect; he looked exactly like a servant of the

1

monolithic KGB, a man who had to stand in the cold if duty dictated, his prey an occupant of the building across the street.

Every detail of his dress and makeup had been worked out with Howard Schmidt, one of the resident geniuses at Amalgamated Press and Wire Services on Dupont circle back in Washington, D.C. The wire service was the front for AXE, the ultrasecret organization originated by David Hawk years earlier at presidential request. Hawk had worked with Bill Donovan in the last days of the OSS, the predecessor to the CIA. He had become the best fieldman of his day and was now acknowledged as the ultimate in secret service chiefs by his peers around the world. His activities were so well disguised, some old colleagues thought he was retired. A few suspected he was heading up a secret group, but not many knew the truth.

And now Hawk's top agent, Nick Carter, designation Killmaster N3, stood in a doorway, thousands of miles from Washington, stamping his frozen feet and watching the windows and entrance across the street, his battered old Zhiguli slowly being covered by snow where it had been parked in haste, now the only car on the street.

As the cold seeped into the marrow of his bones, Carter remembered the last conversation he'd had with Hawk. . . .

"Jamie Fuller is dead," the older man began bluntly, chewing on the end of a soggy cigar.

"Jamie? Hell. I really liked him. How did it happen?" Carter asked.

"We received word from one of our staffers at the embassy. Apparently he went to see a Colonel Yuri Popolov and never returned."

"Popolov . . . Popolov. Isn't he considered a successor to Gregarov?"

"Right. He heads up one of the Chief Directorates. Our man has information that Fuller and Popolov fought to the death," Hawk said, tossing the ruined cigar into a wastebasket and reaching for a fresh one. "It seems that Popolov left some unfinished business that could hurt us badly. We need to know what it is, Nick."

Ginger Bateman, Hawk's longtime secretary, knocked and poked her head in the door. "Howard wants to see Nick before he takes off," she said, smiling at Carter. They'd had something going years earlier but decided it wasn't a good idea. They'd been close friends ever since.

"Thanks, Ginger," Carter said, turning back to Hawk. "I gather you want to find out what Popolov was planning."

Hawk nodded. "It was something big—something about Afghanistan. We can't pass it up, Nick."

Suddenly, all thoughts of Washington and Hawk disappeared as a figure left the building. Carter strained to see through the wind-whipped snow. It was Captain Segorski. The man had finally tired of his mistress and was on his way back to his own bed.

Carter had to move fast. If his target had called for a car, it would be along any minute. He willed his cold limbs to take him to the street corner before the captain. He caught up with him and wasted no time. He moved fast and, with a vicious blow, clipped the lanky younger man from behind, expecting him to fall easily. But the man was warm, his skin and bones resilient, the cloth of his greatcoat too thick for Carter's judo chop to overcome.

The military man turned and faced his attacker. He reached inside his coat for a gun. Carter chopped at his arm with the side of one hand, feeling the jolt vibrate up his arm as the cold of bone and flesh protested. The gun dropped to the snow of the street and was lost. As the Killmaster lunged again, he slipped on the snow.

The captain leveled a blow at Carter's chin, and the AXE agent went down. The Russian was on top of him, throttling him with both hands and cursing into the wind.

No one on the street stopped. No one called out. The man on the bottom was obviously KGB and the other not a member of the common herd. It was not their concern. The few passersby turned their faces out of the wind and walked on, angled bodies churning through a curtain of white on their way to anonymity.

Carter managed a sharp blow to the captain's chin and followed with a knee to the groin. The man slumped in the brown slush thrown up by the few cars that were out.

Carter wasted no time. He reached for the small leather case Schmidt provided on most assignments and filled a small syringe with clear liquid. He stuck the already groaning Russian through the sleeve of his greatcoat with the small syringe. It held a mild tranquilizer that would keep the man from conscious thought for half an hour.

That was the easy part. Now Carter had to learn what the man knew and he didn't have the equipment to do it quickly. He knew of only one place where he could handle the interrogation, but the risk was incredible. AXE, however, didn't pay him to play it safe, he thought.

Carter hoisted the inert man to his shoulder, slipping on the icy pavement, and carried him to the doorway where he'd waited through the long evening. The street was deserted. The snow was falling more heavily than before, coming down in large flakes instead of powder.

Quickly Carter pulled some old clothing from the Zhiguli and replaced the captain's fine Savile Row suit with one of coarse domestic material. He stuffed the body in the back of the small car and hurriedly cleaned off the windshield. After more than an hour in the biting wind, snow had swirled under the hood and covered the motor. It groaned, giving out the grating noise of an almost dead battery. Carter cursed as he tried to coax life into an engine filled with oil that had turned to syrup. It finally caught, coughing, rotating faster before it came fully alive and raced. Slowly, pushing a small snowbank in front of it, the little car headed up the boulevard.

Carter took the bridge across the Moscow River and followed the road that led past the Kremlin, finally coming to Dzerzhinsky Square. The old KGB headquarters building, formerly the headquarters of the All-Russia Insurance Company, stood silently in the blanket of white. Lubyanka Prison occupied all of the right half, the older portion, and all of the basement.

Carter fought the steering wheel of the small car, pulling it through drifts not yet cleared, guiding it to the small parking area at the rear of the prison. He dragged the unconscious captain to a rear door, opened it, and stood inside, dripping slush and water on the tiled floor, holding the man up by one arm.

A guard unslung his submachine gun, a well-used old Kalashnikov, and held it out as a barrier. "Identification," he barked.

Carter produced his KGB identity wallet. Howard Schmidt had given him the rank of major in the dreaded Fifth Department, the Soviet Union's police department responsible for political murders. It was an identity that never failed to send chills down the spine of every comrade, innocent or guilty. "Get me an interrogation room now," he commanded in Russian, flipping the wallet closed and moving forward.

The guard was accustomed to night duty and the interrogation of subversives at any hour. He also knew about the Fifth Department. "Three doors down," he said, fear making his voice unsteady. "Do you need help?" he asked.

"No, I do not need any help," Carter snapped, "and you will make sure I am not disturbed."

The room was about fifteen feet square. It contained one scarred wooden table and two chairs. Against one wall stood a locked cabinet filled with drugs. A few seconds' work with his lockpick and Carter had it open and was reading the labels on the vials. When he found what he wanted, he broke the ampule and filled a syringe.

Carter wasted no time. The inner sanctum of Lubyanka was a frightening place, even more so to one with his experience. You had to know about the torture and killing that had gone on there for years to feel the full impact of fear. The Killmaster knew firsthand the horrors of the place: this was not his first visit. But it was his first as interrogator. He lay the captain on the table, rolled up a sleeve, and inserted the syringe.

It took the powerful drug a minute or two to take effect. Carter looked around. Time permitted no errors, yet he had no time to check for listening devices. The walls were solid. The room had just the one door. No one could observe through one-way glass. This whole action was a massive gamble and one the Killmaster wouldn't have taken if he'd had a choice.

The captain began to move his arms on the table, his hands clawing at the air. His eyes remained closed, but his brow was furrowed.

"State your name," Carter said in Russian, his voice like a whip.

The military man was disoriented. He didn't open his eyes or respond. His limbs stopped moving. Carter slapped his face, hard, first one cheek then the other.

Dulled eyes stared up at him.

"State your name," Carter repeated.

"Se-gor-ski," the man said slowly.

The Killmaster knew the questions would have to follow a slow and natural progression. "Full name?" he asked.

"Vitali Sergeyevich Segorski," the man said, his speech slurred.

"Your rank?" he asked.

"Captain. Twenty-second Spetsnaz."

So the man was an elite soldier, Carter mused. To be in the Spetsnaz was a singular honor. The men were chosen with all the care taken by Delta Force in the States and had the same kind of reputation. If transferred, Segorski would probably make the rank of major immediately.

"You passed on the tip from Popolov. Who did you tell?"

"My father, General Segorski," the captain mumbled.

"His full rank?" Carter asked. He had heard of the general. He should have connected the name.

"General of the Army. Field marshal."

"His command includes the MVD, army intelligence?" Carter asked.

"Yes."

Carter had to speed up the process. Each additional minute of this charade increased his chances of his cover being blown. "Tell me exactly what you told him," he commanded.

The man hesitated before he spoke. He tried to resist the drug but was helpless. "Colonel Yuri Popolov of the KGB planned a raid into Afghanistan soon. He knew the names and locations for the most influential rebel leaders. He planned a kidnapping. Without these men the rebels would be useless against us."

Carter already knew that much. Jamie Fuller had learned of the plan and had forwarded what information he had to Carter's boss. But he didn't know if Popolov was working alone. The West couldn't afford to have the kidnapping take place. Iran and Pakistan would be vulnerable if Afghan resistance ceased, and the whole Persian Gulf would be in danger. Carter's job was to find out if and when it was going to happen.

"How did you learn of Popolov's plan?" he asked.

"He told me."

This was an odd twist. Why the hell would Popolov tell a captain of the Spetsnaz? Carter wondered. Especially the son of the general. "Why would a KGB colonel tell you his plans?" he asked.

"We were becoming friends," the Russian mumbled through lips reluctant to do his bidding.

"Why? Were you spying for your father?" Carter demanded. "If you were, Popolov probably suspected. So why would he tell you? He was no fool."

"I got him drunk. No one except my father knows I learned about the plan."

Carter thought about that for a minute. A KGB colonel letting himself be fed vodka until he told classified military secrets? It didn't seem likely. "Who was close to Popolov?" he asked. "Who was his assistant, his confidant?"

"Alexi Federof was his aide, a major," Segorski said, his voice almost a whisper. His skin was pasty. Sometimes the drug did have side effects, and some subjects were allergic to it. Carter knew he might have very little time left.

"Didn't like him," Segorski went on. "Can't trust him."

This major could be the key, Carter thought. If he was close to Popolov, he might have known his intent. "Where can I find Federof?" he asked.

"Leningrad. Promoted to colonel and sent to Leningrad."

"Wasn't Popolov slated to follow Gregarov as head of the KGB?" Carter asked.

Segorski coughed. He was having some difficulty with his throat. It was constricting on him. "Gregarov didn't like Federof." His voice was a gargle of phlegm. "He kicked him upstairs, but that's as far as he'll ever go. He's had it. No more promotions. Gregarov will have another successor."

The words were coming slowly. The throat was closing, allowing very little breath. A death rattle sounded low in his throat as the door opened and the captain of the prison guard strode in.

"What's the matter with this man?" he asked Carter brusquely. "Who is he?" He was of lower rank than Carter but obviously lord of his domain.

"Political enemy of the state. Unfortunately, sometimes the drug has side effects," Carter replied, trying to keep himself between the captain and the table. "He's had it, but I got what I wanted."

"Your identification, comrade," The captain held out his hand.

Carter produced the wallet. The light was better than in the hall. His makeup had suffered in the hours of frigid weather and the scuffle with Segorski. Time was running out.

The guard glanced at the wallet. He stepped around Carter to look at the man on the table.

"I know that man!" he shouted. "That's Captain Segorski—the general's son. What the hell's going on here?"

Carter didn't waste a second. He chopped the captain across the throat, crushing his larynx, then flipped his wrist to release Hugo, the razor-sharp stiletto he kept in a chamois sheath strapped to his right forearm.

The captain dropped to his knees, his hands to his throat, fighting for his last breath. The veteran guard had his submachine gun cocked and was bringing it around on Carter.

A flash of steel was all the guard saw as he concentrated on getting the Kalashnikov around. The blade buried itself in his throat, severing his jugular, sticking in cartilage as dark blood streamed around it and poured down the man's chest from his neck.

At first the guard didn't move, his face a mask of surprised horror, but finally he fell to his knees. Carter grabbed for his knife as the man toppled over.

The Killmaster opened the door and saw two guards coming from the far end of the hall. Carter had his 9mm Luger in his hand. He had named the well-used gun Wilhelmina long ago when he was younger and more sentimental.

The guards brought up their guns. The Luger barked twice. Neat holes appeared in each of the two foreheads. Blood, brains, and bone splattered on the walls behind them as the slugs exited the backs of their heads.

Carter rushed through the outer door and into the snow that was thicker than ever. His tiny Zhiguli had disappeared under nature's curtain but a Zil limousine had pulled up nearby. Two men were opening the doors.

Carter had wiped Hugo on the captain's tunic and had resheathed it, but the Luger was still in his hand. He slipped the gun into his sleeve and headed toward his own car. When the two men were inside, he turned and ran to the Zil, and managed to hot-wire it and get it under way before the two officers charged out the door firing wildly.

Wind whistled around the small parking lot, blanking out the sound of shots as Carter rounded the corner into the square.

He was a long way from Leningrad.

TWO

An hour of steady driving through the heavy downfall of snow finally brought Carter to the minuscule apartment he had managed to appropriate on Zoologicheskiy Prospekt near the zoo, not far from the West German embassy. He parked the Zil among other identical cars in front of the embassy and managed to gain entry to the ten-by-twenty apartment without the building superintendent's scrutiny.

Schmidt had supplied him with a second cover. He peeled off the KGB disguise, used medical alcohol to wipe his face clean, and donned a neat mustache and beard. In his fine wool greatcoat and black mink hat, he would be an honored member of the National Academy of Science on his way to confer with colleagues.

The Zil was too obvious to use extensively. He drove to the Krasnopresnenskaya metro station, left the Zil, and rode the metro to the Belorusskaya station two stops away. It was adjacent to the Belorussian Station, the terminus of the daily train to Leningrad.

The metro was deserted at this time of night. He was between shifts for factory workers and too early for the thousands who used the line to fill the countless office jobs in

11

the monolith that was the ponderous Russian bureaucracy.

The few unhappy souls on the metro sat dripping snow from wet clothes, staring at the grimy floor beneath their feet, their bodies swaying to the rhythm of the cars. Cleaning women in black coats and woolen scarves held cheap plastic bags on their laps. Men in tattered overcoats and old fur hats dozed and dreamed of better days.

One man was different. Carter spotted him as a minor KGB official, a drone, a cog in the wheel of justice whose job was to observe night traffic for abnormalities. Carter was an abnormality.

"Your identification, comrade," the man said lazily.

Carter passed over the Academy of Science identity card.

"And what is a professor doing on the metro at this time of night?" the small man asked, the indifference changing to insolence.

"I'm off to a conference in Kirov. Nuclear advancement. Very boring, comrade," Carter said through the beard.

"In the middle of the night? I see no baggage," the man sneered. He was smaller than Carter, with a ferretlike face and restless eyes that never stopped in one place for more than a few seconds. He stood over the seated scientist, swaying, his legs braced, as the cars jolted over uneven track.

"I will be met," Carter said. "My luggage will be waiting. The train leaves at dawn."

"I know the schedules and I've heard of no trains leaving at dawn," the man said, sitting next to Carter. "We will get off together and verify your story."

At the cavernous Belorussian Station the KGB man headed for the ticket window, holding Carter by the arm. It was a move typical of the society and an autocratic system that just didn't work. Men and women were assigned at every hour of the day and night to examine anything out of place. Carter was a piece of the wrong jigsaw puzzle.

Before they got to the window, Carter reached for the man's neck and squeezed a junction of nerve endings. Without breaking stride, he took the unconscious man's arm and carried him to the washroom, his feet barely touching the floor.

Like the station, the washroom was deserted. Carter had a problem with disposal. He had to have time to reach Leningrad without an alarm being raised. He hadn't planned on Leningrad, so he didn't know what time the train left or how long the journey took. He could use a powerful drug and put the man out for twenty-four hours or he could terminate him.

He had seen too many dead men that day, so he chose to use Schmidt's kit again, filling a syringe with a potent drug.

As he rolled up the prostrate man's arm, the KGB officer came to life in a flurry of arms and legs. One leg, between Carter's, made a lucky strike. Excruciating pain filled Carter's groin, bringing on a blackout, but before the darkness took him completely, his fist found the other man's jaw.

The blackout was momentary, but the throbbing pain remained. Gingerly, Carter pulled himself from the unconscious man. The washroom was still empty. The syringe had fallen and broken at their feet. Carter prepared another and rammed it home before the small man could give him any more trouble.

When the KGB man was snoring lightly, Carter stepped on a toilet, pulled a heating grate from the wall, stuffed the man inside, and pushed him as far as his arm would reach. Normally it would be a feat of strength he could easily handle. But now it was an act of self-torture. His groin ached unmercifully. He knew he wouldn't be the same for days.

It was almost four in the morning. No one was in the station except a few snoring drunks asleep on wooden benches. Carter asked the ticket woman for Leningrad information. He bought a first-class ticket for the morning train. He had four hours to kill.

It was a milk train. They started a half hour late and were at Bologoye at noon, less than halfway. Men and women sat on long benches, swaying with the motion of the cars, sleeping on each other's shoulders as Carter made his way to find a dining car. He found none.

In his own compartment, which was luxuriously paneled, one other passenger shared the space. A beautiful woman read fashion magazines and kept to herself. She was a brunette, tall and model-slim; Carter guessed she was in her mid-thirties. They had exchanged pleasantries but that was all. Carter had his plans for Leningrad to keep him busy. The woman had her magazines and business papers to occupy her.

As the journey progressed, she looked over her papers more and more often. She was obviously interested in him but, he sensed, not in any personal way. Her scrutiny was cool, almost professional.

When the conductor came for their tickets, the woman had a whispered conversation with him. Within five minutes two burly men, one grossly fat, obviously KGB, entered and demanded identification. They looked alike with broad Slavic faces, dressed all in black.

"You have a question, comrade?" one of the men asked, handing back the woman's identity card.

"This man is wearing a false beard and mustache. They are very good, but they are false," she said, her face expressionless.

One of the men ripped the beard from Carter's face while the other stood with a standard-issue Makarov pistol two feet from Carter's head. They searched him and came up with the Luger and the stiletto. The discovery sent them into a frenzy. A man disguised as a scientist, armed with deadly weapons, was a major find. They had been on train duty for years without such a coup.

The smaller of the two reached for his handcuffs and momentarily covered the line of fire for the gun pointing at Carter. The Killmaster lashed out, catching the first man behind the ear, putting him out. As he turned to the other man, the gun barrel met his skull, sending him to the floor and oblivion.

When Carter came to, the fat man had a pair of handcuffs in his hand. The other sat rubbing his neck.

"How did you suspect, comrade?" the fat man asked, a smile creasing his face as he handcuffed Carter's hands behind his back.

"Wigs, toupées, and theatrical makeup are my business. After years of observing, no false hair can fool me," she announced smugly.

"We will be staying with the prisoner all the way to Leningrad," one of the men told her. "We will have you moved to another compartment."

"No need," she said, an enigmatic smile on her face.

Carter normally didn't resist with a pistol shoved in his face, but this had been different. He couldn't be caught inside Russia. When they knew who he was they'd use everything they knew to interrogate him. And when he had spilled his guts about AXE, his brain would be like a fried egg from the drugs. In the past he'd resisted every known form of torture and never talked. He had the scars to prove it. But that was then and this was now. The new drugs were a different story.

At the moment time was on his side. They had not left the compartment. That meant they had not called ahead announcing their prize catch. They were going to take him in, make a big entrance, impress their peers. Good. *They may be professionals,* Carter thought, *but they're not very bright.*

Carter sat uncomfortably, his hands behind his back, making it impossible to sit in one position for more than a few minutes. His head hurt. His balls hurt. But he would wait. He had more than two hours and he had a plan.

At the end of an hour he stood to get some relief from the handcuffs biting into his wrists. The smaller of the two clubbed him down, raking the barrel of the Makarov across the bridge of his nose.

Blood spurted onto the woman's skirt. She screamed. It was the first emotion she'd shown since the trip began.

"You clumsy oafs!" she cursed. "I'll have to get this stain out right away! Damn you!"

While Carter watched, she pulled a case from a rack and took out another skirt. The compartment had a small washroom. She changed her skirt out of their sight, washed out the bloodstain, and hung it up to dry over the sink.

"Put the handcuffs in front," Carter suggested. "I can't sit for another hour like this."

"We have our orders. You stay as you are."

"But dammit—"

"Two men with guns can't let him sit handcuffed in front?" the woman scoffed, shaming them. "Members of our vaunted KGB are cowards? And why aren't you wiping the blood from his face? It makes me sick."

Carter had gauged the woman correctly. He had counted on her intervention.

The two men looked at each other. Carter enjoyed the indecision. The rules were absolute. But in the face of a beautiful woman who ridiculed them . . . ?

"We have orders. You saw him attack."

"Cowards."

"You can be moved to another compartment."

"No. This is my compartment, comrades. Move if you want to. I'm staying," she said with finality.

They looked at each other and shrugged. One sat opposite Carter with the oversize gun in his hand pointed at his gut. The other moved the handcuffs to Carter's front and pocketed the key.

"What about the blood?" the woman asked.

Carter solved it for them. "I have to use the toilet," he announced.

"All right," the man with the gun said, moving over to cover the washroom door. "Keep the door open."

"What about the woman?" he asked, pointing his manacled hands her way.

"Don't worry about me," she said. "You're better entertainment than the fashion magazines."

Carter moved to the small washroom and awkwardly washed the blood from his face. He took his time. He turned and unzipped his fly, managing to face the toilet, turn his body away from the open door, and convey a general attitude of acute embarrassment at the same time.

His hands were hidden from view as he slowly peeled an egg-sized gas bomb—the third of the trio of weapons Carter invariably carried—from an inner thigh. His testicles were tender and bruised. The least contact with them was painful. He tried to remember whether he had selected a lethal bomb or one that would just knock out everyone who breathed the gas. He remembered it was not a lethal one.

Before unscrewing the two halves of the bomb and letting its gas escape, Carter went over what he had to do. Through long years of yoga training, he could hold his breath for four minutes. He had to restore his clothing, find the key to the handcuffs, and get away. He knew he could get out of the compartment with the handcuffs on and come back later, but how could he explain them if seen by others on the train?

The gas normally dissipated in six or seven minutes, but it might last longer in the small, close compartment.

He unscrewed the two halves, held his breath, and tossed the bomb on the floor at the men's feet. He zipped up his pants. The men sat, stunned, breathing in the gas, their faces registering surprise and shock as they felt their lungs burn.

They fell. The largest of the two fell on the smaller, the one with the key. Carter dragged him off and turned to the other, kneeling awkwardly, turning him over to find the right pocket.

The woman sat staring at him. She had held her breath. Her eyes bulged. One hand reached out for the fallen gun.

Carter knew he couldn't let her move further. He chopped her on the side of her neck and she sucked air, losing consciousness with a look of anger on her face.

Two minutes.

Carter fumbled in the pocket he'd seen the man use, but the key wasn't there. It was difficult rummaging around with both hands in small pockets. He cursed aloud. The little man had moved it.

Carter considered walking into the corridor and taking his

chances. He tried the other pockets and finally found the key in a breast pocket.

Three minutes.

He fitted the key in the lock, his own lungs starting to burn. The handcuffs came free. He tossed them on the seat and headed for the door, opening it fast and closing it just as fast.

He took a deep breath of fresh air.

"You!"

He turned to find the conductor staring at him, eyes wide. They were alone in the corridor.

Carter had no choice, no time for fancy solutions. He chopped at the man's neck, caught him, opened the compartment door, and shoved him in.

THREE

The room in the cheap hotel looked out on the waterfront. It was a dreary day. The snow had stopped but the streets were clogged. Most of the people Carter could see were on foot. Vehicles were bogged down. Scores of dockhands, out of work since the harbor froze over, were shoveling vehicles free or making pathways for deliveries to the few ships stranded in port.

Carter went back to the bed and sat, flaming a bitter local cigarette, wishing he had some of his own custom blends. He was in a foul mood. This job was going poorly. He had part of the puzzle, but the rest, the real cream, was eluding him. He felt sure that Colonel Federof had the answers. The man had been close to Popolov. It was possible he had not told all he knew. If he didn't, all of this was for nothing.

Carter thought for a moment about the day before. He'd left the train with the occupants of his compartment sound asleep. He'd given them all a shot to keep them out another twenty-four hours. As soon as he'd left the train, he'd discarded the finery of the scientist for a pea jacket and wool cap of the typical Russian sailor and taken the room. He had no idea how he was going to get to Federof. You just don't walk up to the head of the KGB for Leningrad and start asking questions.

19

• • •

KGB headquarters was an old building inland on Dashkov
Place. Carter spent a couple of days studying the movements
of officers coming and going. He had pegged Federof on the
second day and followed him in an old car he had stolen an
hour earlier. The AXE agent was playing it on the edge. The
KGB chief was never without guards. Anyone loitering near
the building was suspect. The stolen car was a risk in a town
with so few cars on the streets. To make it worse, the snow
made life miserable for everyone. The bitter cold forced its
way to the bone, even in one as fit as he. Wherever he went,
Carter found everyone in a sour mood and he was beginning
to feel the same way.

The chauffeured Zil, black and shiny against the white of
the streets, was always occupied by three men, a driver, two
guards, and Federof. Carter made the round trip to the
colonel's house three times before he was sure they always
took the same route. He abandoned the car and walked back
to his shabby room to lay on the bed and stare up at the cracked
ceiling.

He had no resources other than his weapons. Somewhere
along the line he'd lost the small drug case Schmidt had
provided. What would be the best way to get at Federof . . . ?

Patience. He was rushing things. If the Russians planned a
kidnapping in Afghanistan, it would take time to set up. He'd
just have to be patient.

Two nights later the Zil changed the pattern. Federof was
driven to a large house on Zubo Street and dropped off. The car
continued with the guards still inside.

Carter parked another nondescript car he'd stolen two
blocks away and walked back to the house. It was surrounded
by a high fence. Lights shone on all floors. Guards could be
seen at the front and back. On a balmy summer night anywhere
in the world, getting inside wouldn't be easy. But here, at
twenty below zero, with the wind blowing in off the Gulf of
Finland, Carter cursed his luck.

The cold steel fence claimed his gloves in a vise of frost as he climbed up and over. By the time he was in the grounds he'd lost some of the skin from the palms of his hands. They were blue with cold but wouldn't start to hurt until later.

It wasn't any better for the guards. Their breath fogged their vision and frosted the edges of their parkas. They walked their posts like robots, their brains as numb as their feet.

Carter flipped Hugo into an almost frostbitten palm and took the first guard from behind. The man went up on his toes as the long blade penetrated to his heart. As he died, Carter hooked him on the old-fashioned ironwork surrounding the door so that he faced the street, the rifle still in his hands.

He knew he had to hurry. The cold was slowing his motions, the air painful to breathe. His hands were like steel claws almost unwilling to do his bidding.

The snow crunched under his feet as he made his way to the back door. It was more than a crunch. The crusted snow seemed alive and protested as he stepped on it, squeaking in annoyance as he moved.

The guard at the door swung around. They were ten feet apart. Everything seemed to be in slow motion. Carter could see the man's finger tighten on the trigger. The firing pin made a loud metallic sound as it came down on an empty chamber.

Carter didn't wait to think about his good luck. He should have been a dead man, dead and stiff in the cold of a hostile city. But he was not. Swiftly and silently, he drove the blade of his knife up and into the man's breastbone.

The fight wasn't over. The blade had not pierced the heart. It had missed the aorta, glanced off a rib, and penetrated a lung. Red froth foamed from the square face as the guard brought his rifle up in a savage blow. The pea jacket took most of the shock, but the tenderness had still not left his groin and the pain almost knocked Carter out.

He withdrew his knife and plunged it home again. The man's eyes glazed as he fell forward, a dead weight in Carter's arms.

They slid down to the back stoop together, both on their knees, one dead, the other breathing hard.

Slowly the pain eased and the stars stopped flashing in Carter's head. He released the body and let it fall to one side. Painfully he rose to his feet, the bloody knife still in his hand.

The door was locked. He used Hugo to snap the bolt and found himself in an outer shell, an anteroom used only in winter. He looked through a frosted window. Two people were working in a kitchen. He rapped on the window and shouted for them to let him in.

Unsuspecting, sure the racket was from the frozen guard outside, the man ambled to the door, opened it, and went back to his chores without seeing Carter on the threshold.

"Are you the only ones in the house with the colonel?" he asked, shivering.

They turned as one. The woman held her hand to her mouth, gasping in fright. Carter still held the bloody knife. His hands were raw and dripping blood as the warmth of the kitchen began to thaw them.

The man spoke first, his voice reflecting his fear. "Don't hurt us. Please. We are nobody."

"Answer the question," Carter said, "and you won't be hurt." The heat of the kitchen was starting to get to him. Every extremity ached, and his groin throbbed where he was bruised. "Who else is here?" he asked.

"Two guards outside," the man said haltingly, "and one at the foot of the stairs."

"Who is upstairs?"

"The colonel and our mistress."

"In bed?" Carter asked.

The woman said nothing, but lowered her eyes.

"Probably," the man replied.

"How long has he been upstairs?"

"An hour, maybe less. We take them some refreshments in an hour."

"Call the guard in here," Carter ordered.

"He won't come," the man said.

Carter looked at the woman. She had fine features and a ripe figure. With some makeup and beter clothes she would be attractive, he thought.

"Call the guard," he repeated.

"I won't," she said, bringing her chin up stubbornly.

"You asked me not to hurt you," Carter said, waving his knife at the man. "You won't be hurt if she does as I say."

The man nodded at his wife, fear evident in his gesture.

Timidly she went to the door and called for the guard, but nothing happened. The guard didn't move.

She called again, putting more urgency in her voice, and they could hear the heavy footfalls of the guard come their way.

Carter motioned her to the center of the room. He stood behind the door.

As the guard entered, his back to the intruder, Carter brought the butt end of his Luger down on the man's head. The guard staggered, held his head for a moment, and went down.

Carter tied the couple's hands and feet and locked them in a pantry. As he turned, the guard, on his feet and groggy, swung his rifle in a desperate arc that caught the man from AXE on the side of his thigh. Pain rocketed up his side and to his groin. The shock had jolted every aching joint and particularly his crotch.

The guard wasn't really conscious of his actions, standing unsteadily in the middle of the room. Carter hit him again with the gun, tied him, and shoved him in the pantry with the others.

The house was solid and quiet, deathly quiet. Carter took a minute to concentrate on the job ahead and shut out the pain of the frost still escaping his limbs and the throbbing pain of his groin.

The house was a square plan, the stairs to the upper floors in the middle of the house solid oak, polished and carpeted. They made no noise as he ascended. He reached the top step and stopped to listen. He could see five doors. Any one could hold trouble.

With Hugo in his left hand and Wilhelmina in his right, he

crept along the hall to the right until he heard a keening noise. It was the woman. His timing had been perfect. Something finally had to go right on this assignment, he thought. She was at the height of her passion. The colonel and his lady were about as preoccupied as they could get.

Carter eased open the door. It was her bedroom, warmer than the rest of the house. A huge bed stood in the center of the room. The scents of lavender and dusting powder were overpowered by the smell of human sweat.

The colonel was above his mistress, long legs, white as the snow outside the house, wrapped around him.

Carter closed the door and wasted a few precious minutes. When their lovemaking was over and they had settled down, he moved quickly, his knife in his hand. He didn't give them time to react. As he stood before them, his knife an inch from the man's throat, his mind recorded the details. They were two healthy animals in their mid to late thirties. The woman was beautiful, pale and blue-eyed, her hair a shimmering blond curtain the color of wheat. The man was well muscled, square-jawed. He had dark hair. The eyes that shone in hatred were black.

By the time they had recovered, even slightly, he had moved to stand behind the headboard. He had the gun at the woman's throat and the stiletto piercing the flesh below the man's ear.

"Who the hell are you?" the man bellowed. "You're a dead man, you hear? A dead man!"

"It doesn't matter who I am, Federof. The only thing that matters is whether you will survive."

He could see that the woman was about to scream.

"Quiet!" he shouted at her. "No one's around to hear you, but we'll keep it quiet anyway."

Carter could see her abdomen expand and contract as if she were hyperventilating, but nothing came from her mouth. She was convulsing in silent fear.

"What . . . do you want?" the man asked. His voice showed real fear for the first time.

"You answer my questions and you will live. You don't answer my questions and you will die. It's easy."

The man was silent for a moment as if thinking.

"What's so important?" the man asked.

"You are Colonel Alexei Federof, yes?" Carter asked.

"You knew that before you came in here."

Carter pressed the knife behind Federof's ear. "Just answer the question."

"Yes," Federof screamed in pain.

"You were Colonel Popolov's aide?"

"Yes."

"All right," Carter said, shifting his position. He kept the knife in place but eased the Luger from the woman. "Popolov told Segorski, the son, about the plot to kidnap Afghan rebel leaders. Why?"

"Did he have . . . to have a reason?" the colonel choked out through the pain.

"Don't be funny!" Carter snapped, pressing the knife again. "Does the KGB talk to the MVD? No way. Popolov *wanted* Segorski to tell his father. Am I right?"

"Yes."

"Why? He had to know the old man would run with the plot. If General Anatole Segorski knew of a plot by the KGB to kidnap the Afghan leaders, he'd be there first."

"That was the idea," Federof said, his voice almost a whisper. A trickle of blood ran down the knife to Carter's skinned hand and to the sheet.

"Explain," Carter said, keeping his voice steady, but as menacing as ever.

The woman made a move to squirm away from the gun barrel. "Don't!" he commanded. "You'll just make it worse for him."

The blade had penetrated another fraction of an inch while he dealt with the woman. Federof had passed out, and the woman, too, had fainted from terror.

Carter walked to a table against one wall. It was a large room. The huge bed took up the middle, while the table and various divans and overstuffed chairs lined the walls. A jug of water and some glasses stood on a tray on the table.

Carter poured the water over Federof's head. The Russian spluttered and wiped his hands over his face. The woman was still out, her mouth slack, her breasts rising and falling with a steady cadence.

Carter moved to the foot of the bed, his Luger pointed at the man's head. He asked the question again.

"Explain. Why would Popolov pass on such information?"

The answer came from a man almost incoherent with fear. No guards had come to help. He had never been without backup before. "Gregarov and Segorski . . . are bitter enemies. The head of the . . . KGB and the Field Marshal of the Army . . . have been after the First Minister's job for years. Popolov's . . . Popolov's plot wasn't the first."

"Get to the point. Gregarov was Popolov's boss and now he's yours. So he knows about it. I don't see the problem."

"But he . . . he doesn't know . . . know all the facts. Popolov was killed before he got to Gregarov."

"So Gregarov doesn't know all the facts. What's the complication?"

Carter was getting impatient. Someone could come any second. What the hell was the point? He still didn't get it.

"Popolov knew . . . he knew the scheme would probably backfire," Federof went on, his body shaking, his teeth chattering. "He made . . . somehow he made sure it wouldn't work. It has to fail . . . some mechanism or someone, I think maybe an ally in Afghanistan, is in place to make it fail. So the whole thing was a disinformation plot . . . something to set up General Segorski."

"But Popolov died too soon and Gregarov thinks it will work. So he's going to beat the general to the scene. Is that it?"

"My chief—Gregarov—doesn't know . . . doesn't know that Popolov schemed to make the plan fail . . . something he's set up . . . in Afghanistan . . . to screw up the general. Gregarov will fall into the . . . the same trap," Federof said, his voice barely audible.

"Why didn't *you* tell Gregarov?"

"I didn't know all of it. Yuri Popolov was Gregarov's pet . . . the one who would . . . one day . . . succeed him."

"Not exactly right. Gregarov wasn't about to make you his heir and you left him to his fate, to whatever Popolov set up. Isn't that it?" Carter demanded.

"Gregarov can . . . go to . . . go to hell. I don't care."

Carter stared down the sight of the gun at the man and analyzed the facts. If Gregarov of the KGB and Segorski of the MVD both sent expeditions to kidnap the Afghan rebel leaders, it might work out best for his people. But what was the monkey wrench, the surprise that Popolov had thrown into the works?

It was better that Gregarov didn't know all the facts. And only one man could tell him. Carter took a deep breath, pulled back the hammer, and put a 9mm slug through Federof's head.

Blood splattered the woman. She opened her eyes and screamed. Then her face went slack and she passed out again.

FOUR

The suite on Elmsta Street was a far cry from the shabby little room he'd occupied in Leningrad. It was in a five-star hotel. The upholstery and carpeting were the very finest. The pictures on the walls were original oil paintings. Gold faucets adorned onyx sinks in the bathroom. The sunken tub with Jacuzzi could easily accommodate two.

Carter reached for a cigarette, flamed it, and crawled out of bed. He stood at the window and looked out at the palace between the hotel and the harbor. Stockholm was blanketed with snow. Ships were at rest in the harbor. Here, in a kingdom that was as much of a democracy as any, he felt the healthy fear of the Russian bear melt from him.

He had called Hawk a few hours earlier. The old man had promised to call back and let him know how they were affected. He had been pleased with the job, told Carter to relax, to get rid of the tension and enjoy himself.

The hotel doctor had given him something for his hands. They weren't bandaged. The salve, one of the sulfa antiburn remedies, had done a miraculous job. So had the woman.

Olga. She was the daughter of a very rich shipping magnate. He had met her in the bar downstairs and she'd been just what he needed. She was beautiful, elegant, and spoke excellent

29

English. They'd enjoyed each other's company over drinks, and one thing led to another. He turned to look at her stretched out on the bed like a snow cat resting after a feast.

Her long white-blond hair was what he'd noticed first. Now it fell across the pillow and ribbed her face like cascading sunlight. The tuft of hair at her groin was darker and curlier. Bereft of the sun's rays and the care she obviously lavished on her long tresses, it was duller.

Olga was tall and slim, but she had soft, full breasts, and a well-shaped derriere. Her thighs and legs were strong, like a dancer or athlete. With all she had going for her, Olga's eyes were her best feature. They were the color of the Caribbean, so clear a blue-green you swore you could see through them into her soul.

She turned on the bed, her legs spread. Her eyes opened. She smiled and languidly held out her arms to him. She was incredible. They had made love for hours and she wanted more.

He crushed out the cigarette and went to her. She was his Viking goddess, his spirit of the cold northern forests, but her flesh was warm as she pressed herself to him. She wrapped her long legs around him and held him as close as she could, murmuring into her ear, her voice a whisper as she slid one hand down to grasp and caress him.

The hand was like fire that would engulf him. As he filled it, her motion continued until she knew it was time. She guided him to her, her hand forming a ring around him as he slid into her.

They lay still, each cell alive as it touched another, alive and pulsing, ready to perform, to experience sensation as never before.

She started to move first. Slowly. The movement was almost imperceptible, but as each second passed, a new awareness built with a cumulative effect that sent the senses reeling, screaming for relief.

And it had just begun.

He started to move faster, driven by a compulsion to feel more. His body burned with sensation. It was as if she were a furnace that held him, prepared him for a heaven or a hell that he would never forget.

Her eyes were open and he looked into their aquamarine depths as she moved beneath him. Then she closed her eyes and brought her mouth to his, sucking at his lips, forcing her tongue into his mouth, demanding and hot. She was on fire from head to toe and transmitted the heat to him like a living thing.

He couldn't hold back. Her pace was driving him forward so quickly he could hardly breathe. It was as if he were on a carnival ride controlled by a madman.

He moved faster within her and the sensation increased. She called out as a wave of passion hit her. She called out to him again, then started a whispered moaning as her fulfillment became constant, one wave of pure pleasure, the prize she had been seeking for both of them.

He churned with her, feeling all the sensations she had built within him coming to the surface, concentrating to attack him at one point, funneling to the center of his being and rushing on an irreversible course to the place where they were joined. Then, when he thought he could not possibly go faster without dying, he let go.

Their breaths were ragged as they descended to a lower plateau. Sweat glistened on their skin as they still rocked together, but ever slower, until they held each other in one long, contented sigh.

And it was over.

She held him close as if she were afraid he'd disappear. He leaned back and looked into the depths of those beautiful eyes, seeing the inner woman, the loneliness and the hunger.

The green eyes closed. Her breathing became slow and even. Her arms released him as she slept.

He slipped from her, rolled to the other side of the bed, and lit another cigarette.

He thought about their earlier meeting at the bar downstairs. His mind drifted back to the hours before, the last minutes in Leningrad, the last hours. . . .

Federof was dead. The colonel had told him all he could, but it was enough. Now he had the whole story, or as much of it as he was going to get there. He had what Hawk wanted and he probably had the solution. The only part of the mystery was Popolov's ringer, the scheme the dead KGB man had cooked up to ensure that Anatole Segorski failed. Even with his experience, he found it difficult to imagine a plot that would have one man kill off a whole expedition of his own people to gain political advantage.

He forced himself to hurry to take care of the business at hand. Federof's mistress was unconscious, probably in shock. He found her robe, tore it into strips, and tied her hand and foot. Then he shoved a bit of the cloth in her mouth and tucked her away in a closet to give himself time to get clear. He had to get out of Russia. But where? And how?

He moved from the bed and rifled through Federof's desk. He found a passport and papers that Federof had used a year earlier—exactly one year before. Carter never believed in coincidences, but he figured he was due for some extraordinary good luck.

He found a magnifying glass in the desk and an assortment of pens. He practiced the forgery on a blank pad for a few minutes, and carefully changed the digit.

It was done. Now he had to look like Federof. They were of similar build, and Federof's uniform fitted him well.

He went to the bathroom, stripped down, showered, and shaved. Their hair and eyes were similar. It was the squared face that was the problem. Carter stuffed some cotton between his teeth and gums and got the effect he wanted. He dressed, donned a pair of sunglasses, and examined himself in the mirror. He would pass except for the hands. He found a pair of gloves and gingerly pulled them on.

He picked up the phone at Federof's bedside and called the airport.

"Ticket information."

"Colonel Alexei Federof, KGB. My fool secretary forgot to call for my tickets. I must be in London tomorrow." He looked at his watch. It was two in the morning. "Wait. That's today. I must be there today."

"We have a flight out at seven o'clock this morning, but I'm afraid it's fully booked."

"Then you will bump someone. It is imperative I be there today. Comrad Gregarov has demanded it."

"The ticket will be waiting. Please be here one hour before flight time."

Carter put down the receiver and sat for a minute trying to come up with a better plan. He could drive to Pulkovo International Airport in less than an hour. He had no idea what would be happening here, at this house. When were the guards relieved? Did he have time to get to the airport and in the air before the bodies were discovered?

What about when he was airborne? They could always turn the plane around.

Carter decided that worrying was pointless. He'd have to get moving and play it by ear.

The woman's car was a Mercedes 450. He drove it within the speed limit across town and to the approaches to Pulkovo. He went to the ticket counter. They had his ticket set aside.

He had two hours to kill. He went to the bar, a dingy hole at the far end of the corridor leading to his departure ramp. It wasn't very inviting, but it was dark and away from the main part of the terminal.

The bar was almost empty. He nursed three drinks over the hour. The only other traveler was a garrulous engineer off to Sweden, a man so excited about his first trip out of the Soviet Union that he thought nothing of striking up a friendly conversation with a KGB colonel. The big man, who introduced himself as Serge Bresnikov, kept up a steady chatter.

His plane left fifteen minutes later than Carter's .

Bresnikov had only one redeeming feature. He looked like Carter. If he hadn't been such a nonstop talker, Carter might have enjoyed whiling away the time with him.

At six, Carter picked up his small bag and headed for the departure gate. The atmosphere of the airport had changed. Military police were everywhere. They were stopping and examining every military man.

That meant only one thing: Federof had been found.

He returned to the bar. It was deserted except for his motor-mouth lookalike.

"Serge. Another drink? My plane has been delayed."

"I'm going to leave soon myself," the engineer said, "but what the hell? One more won't hurt."

They had another vodka, the engineer still babbling a mile a minute. The bartender had gone to a supply room. They were alone.

Carter reached past Serge as if he were getting a paper napkin, then, on the way back he pressed his hand against Serge's temple for a few seconds. When his companion was unconscious, Carter carried him to the bar's small rest room.

The Killmaster exchanged clothing with the man in record time. It was quarter to seven. He examined the other man's papers. Serge Mikail Bresnikov was from Kiev, an engineer from the National Engineering Institute. It would do. He shoved Federof's papers in the greatcoat and was about to leave with the other man's bag when a thought occurred to him.

Bresnikov would tell his name and destination when he regained consciousness. At first they would give him a hard time, but they would check. And they would turn the Stockholm plane around. Apprehending Federof's murderer warranted any action.

Reluctantly Carter pulled Federof's gun from its holster and swung it hard against the man's temple. He felt for a pulse. It was weak and ragged. The man wouldn't die, but he wouldn't give them any information for days. Carter lifted the man's head and smeared the edge of the toilet with blood. He might have slipped and fallen in the none-to-clean enclosure.

The bar was still deserted. Carter made his way to the departure area. It was five to seven. The London plane was still being held. The Stockholm plane was to leave in twenty minutes.

Carter sidled up to the officer in charge. He tried to get his attention, but it wasn't easy. The man was impossible, completely ignoring civilians. With just fifteen minutes to his flight departure, he pulled at the man's sleeve.

"Something strange in the washroom of the bar, comrade. A trickle of blood from a booth and the bottom of an officer's coat showing beneath the door."

All hell broke loose. Whistles sounded. All attention was on the officer as he charged down the corridor with all his men following.

Carter slipped past the security check, turned in Bresnikov's ticket, and was on board five minutes before takeoff. He sat next to an elderly Swedish woman who dozed all the way to Stockholm.

. . . The sound of the telephone on the bedside table brought Carter back to the present. He picked it up. Only one person could be calling.

"Nick? You there? What the hell's going on?"

Carter checked the bed. Olga was sleeping, or appeared to be. He moved to the far corner of the room, dragging the cord after him, and cupped his hand around the transmitter. "Nothing. I'm with you," he said to Hawk. "Well, what did they say?"

"It's still ours. I want you in Afghanistan as soon as possible. Our people think the Soviets won't get to the final showdown for weeks, but we want you there now."

He looked at Olga and saw her eyes open. "I'll get the first flight out tomorrow. That'll give me time to snoop around Kabul."

"What's your plan once you get there? I've had input on the

kidnap plot from another source. We've already started the ball rolling in Kabul."

"Good. Get someone to pick up my weapons at the American consulate here and drop them in Kabul."

"We don't have a consulate in Afghanistan."

"I know that, and that's Smitty's problem. That's why he's your Operations chief. Tell him I said to start earning his salary," Carter chuckled.

"What's your plan for Kabul?" Hawk asked again.

"Before Jamie Fuller killed him, Popolov arranged something that would screw up General Segorski. To be effective, it's got to originate in Kabul." Carter had walked to the window, trailing the long cord, and was looking out on the city.

"You plan to infiltrate staff headquarters?" the gruff voice asked.

"Something like that."

"The Afghan targets are Amin and Haami. Hafi Amin and Jalaludin Haami are the only ones the rebels really trust. The other so-called leaders are all lining their pockets. Only about twenty percent of our aid gets to the fighting men."

"So what else is new?"

"Amin has a son, Salman, who is his right-hand man. Haami's daughter Odah is one of the *Mujaheddin*. I'd hate to see anything happen to them while you're there."

"An Afghan woman freedom fighter? That's unusual. How does she get around all the taboos of their faith?" Carter asked, intrigued.

"They tell me she's an unusual one, flaunts convention and gets away with it. I want you to watch yourself around her."

"An Afghan woman? Are you kidding? I know how their men feel about that. I'm off to Kabul tomorrow. They might still have open lines for international calls. I'll try to keep you informed through the computer."

"Wait," Hawk commanded. "I don't usually tell you how to do your job, but this one is different."

"In what way?"

"You're going into a war zone. You're posing as a Soviet officer part of the time," Hawk said, his words punctuated by breathing that could only come from puffing on one of his foul-smelling cigars. "I don't want you playing war games."

"You know I—"

"You'll be tempted, Nick. It's only natural. I want Nick Carter working for me, not General Patton. Clear enough?"

Carter felt like a schoolboy being chastised by the headmaster. But he knew Hawk was right.

"I'll remember, sir," he said.

When he turned from the window to hang up, Olga was smiling. She moved sensually on the bed, her silken hair falling over her breasts, and held her arms out to him.

He walked slowly toward those outstretched arms, all thoughts of Afghanistan temporarily forgotten.

FIVE

Jalaludin Haami sat alone in the cave his men had carved
out of a canyon wall a few miles from Khost, the regional
military headquarters for the Soviet Red Army. The mountain
ranges, row on row, paralleled the border with Pakistan. They
were rugged and barren, cold at night and too close to the sun
during the day.

The solemn man sat cross-legged, a submachine gun across
his lap, a cup of his morning tea in his right hand.

Haami was a short man and thin, his face, always solemn,
was full-bearded, the black facial hair straight and long to the
middle of his chest. He wore a loose shirt and baggy pants in
battleship gray, the standard garb for all his men. It looked like
a poorly tailored safari suit. His turban, twelve yards of cotton
twill, white with a wide checked design of black lines, was
wound around his head, the tail falling over his left shoulder.
Haami's skin was light, toughened but not browned by years
of outdoor camps. His eyes, as black as outer space, looked sad
as they stared straight ahead.

Haami wasn't alone. Another man sat near him. He sat
silent, allowing the leader the luxury of private thoughts. He
was an American, a huge, muscular, completely bald black

man who fought with them, ate with them, and emulated their customs. He had been trained in the U.S. army, had come there out of faith, faith in the cause of the Afghan, a love of Allah, and a hatred of what the Soviet Union was doing to this country. He had been invaluable in training the undisciplined tribesmen. They had all learned from him. He told them his name was Ahmed Shah. If he had an American, non-Muslim name, they never learned it.

"I have never told you of the early years," the older man began.

"I know some of it, but my history is sketchy," the American admitted.

"I sometimes wonder where it all went wrong," Haami said wistfully. "We were the worst kind of fools when we were younger, and naïve. We hadn't seen it coming," he went on. "It started so slowly . . . so subtly. We were babes compared to our enemy, the men of the cunning black bear."

"They probably didn't intend to show their hand," Shah said.

Haami's thoughts went back to 1967. Twenty-one years. He'd been about thirty-five. He remembered how the music blared, how the bright lights and fireworks flared in the capital of Kabul as his fellow Afghans celebrated forty-eight years of full independence. Yet with the winds of the cold war already blowing to the north, Soviet tanks and rocket launchers rumbled along Aknar Khan Street and MIGs screamed overhead to highlight the military parade. He also recalled with irony that at the time, the philosophy, the excuse for their courtship and rape, had been beautifully Afghan: "When you ride a beautiful horse," they had proclaimed, "do you care in which country it was born?"

"That was how it was," he explained to the big American. "Fools! We were fools!"

He remembered with bile rising to his throat that by 1979, the regime ruling Afghanistan was Soviet-controlled. He and many men like him, simple men of peace, had protested, had waited too long, and had finally taken up arms. In the tumult of the first armed resistance to the regime, Afghan's revolutionary president, his friend Hafizullah Akbar, suspected of making overtures to the West, was assassinated. It had hurt. Oh, how the deaths of his friends had hurt!

"Then the whores to the north had really taken hold," he explained to Ahmed Shah. "The U.S. ambassador Adolph Dubs died along with thousands of innocent Afghans as the Red Army, eighty thousand strong, rolled over the border."

He stopped for a moment, choked with emotion. "It was the worst kind of pain . . . the watching, the feeling of helplessness.

"So we took up arms, but look at us now," he recalled with sadness. "The dead on both sides have piled up like cordwood. The *Mujaheddin*, our gallant fighting men, have been pushed back and confined to the hills around Gardez and Paktia near the border of Pakistan. I sometimes think my leadership has failed, that I should turn the job over to the younger men."

"You know that isn't so," Shah said, touching the older man's shoulder gently. "We are close to the government stronghold of Khost, and for the first time in five years we have it under a siege that is working."

Haami listened to the praise without emotion. He was riddled with doubts. It wasn't the men. He was proud of his men. They constituted a formidable force on the ground, but they had no air support or heavy equipment. They were like an army with only one arm.

In the weeks just past, Allah, bless His name, had been good to them. A Soviet strike force, led by heavy transport jets, protected by MIG-21s, had flown into Khost determined to break the rebel's stranglehold on the hills along the Pakistani border.

The Soviet army lost its battle before it began. Haami was proud of the Afghan people and their allegiance to truth. Under the leadership of Marxist Babrak Kharma, the force of more than ninety thousand men had shrunk to a third its size. Good men, Afghans, had deserted from government to rebel camps. He knew that some, and who could blame them, simply went home. Haami recalled the result with a rare smile

creasing his face. Entire army units surrendered along with
their Soviet T-55 tanks and MI-24 helicopters, all operated by
Afghan regulars.

He had been expressing his thoughts to the attentive young
American. "I have no pity for the invaders," he went on. "May
Allah damn them for eternity. He is helping us in many ways.
The Soviet leaders, far from home, are frustrated by mass
desertions of local troops. Their leaders are enraged by the
growing use of drugs and alcohol by their own men, the young
Russians conscripted to come here," he said. It was typical of
the man that he was as sad for the young Russians as he was
for his own people. They didn't want to fight any more than
did his countrymen. "I've received intelligence that they've
decided to take drastic action," he went on. "Something new
is being planned, something with more finesse. My spies have
uncovered an undercurrent, but they had no details."

In the distance the two men could hear artillery exchanges.
The battle for Khost had resumed. Higher up in the range
above them, along the cliffs and mountain trails leading from
Pakistan, caravans of camels and donkeys were in constant
procession, carrying arms from Pakistan.

Below them, spread out in a small valley, thousands of their
men went about the business of war, cleaning weapons,
drinking tea, and talking through the day, until the time came
for battle.

Around the hills, to their left and right, and in caves higher
than the one they used, men squatted at their few pitiful
antiaircraft gun emplacements, on guard for the raids of Soviet
MI-24 gunships that must inevitably come.

Haami and his people had planned well. Caches of arms
were buried in the hills in every direction. The caravans from
Pakistan never ceased.

The rebel leader had stopped talking for the moment. The
two men sat in silence. The fire at their feet had gone out. The
tea was cold. Memories of past mistakes left Haami with a
feeling of defeat he seldom allowed himself. His shoulders
drooped uncharacteristically.

It was the American black man who broke the silence. "It's their planned cold-blooded acts that surprise me," he said. "To kill or ship out every medic is about as dirty as you can play the game."

"When a member of a family is ill, the whole family has to emigrate to Pakistan. Few return," Haami said sadly.

"And the destruction of the mosques," Shah went on bitterly. "The Soviet bastards have destroyed all our mosques."

"*Our* mosques?" Haami said, grinning.

"You mock me, friend. I have been one of you for months."

"I do not mock, my friend. Your loyalty and help have inspired most of us. We also bleed for the systematic destruction of our country. Only the infrastructure the Soviets will need is not destroyed—the roads, water, communication. The hospitals are gone, and the schools. I'm convinced they are stupid."

The crunch of gravel to his right alerted the leader to an intruder. In the midst of his own camp his hand went to his rifle, a reaction as natural as breathing. The younger man had a submachine gun pointed at the source of the noise.

"Father—are you going to shoot your own flesh and blood?" a female voice, alive with laughter, rang out to him like tinkling bells.

In the midst of Allah's furnace, in the crucible of this holy war, Odah, his daughter, had come to him. Against all the laws of Islam this one carried a gun, led a platoon, refused to wear a veil. Worse, she wore the shirt and pants of the peasant fighter, showing off her charms like the whores of Cairo.

But she was the light of his life. She had also proved to be one of his best fighters and a natural leader. With all his sons dead and his wife at their home camp, this one was his only source of peace. So while he didn't approve, he rejoiced at her presence.

Ahmed Shah moved away from them as the young woman squatted at her father's side. She was as tall as her father, wore the same kind of turban, carried a similar rifle. Except for the smooth face, the face of an angel, she was not unlike the others.

"You have been thinking of the past again," she said gently.

"Know your past to make sure of your future," he said, his voice taking on the gentle quality reserved for her. "How is the preparation?"

"It goes on. As always it goes on."

"Don't be a cynic, Odah. This siege will work. We have never been in better shape."

"It's not this siege, father," she said, her lilting voice a rose in the midst of thorns. " It's the futility. Taking Khost is like scratching a flea bite when the enemy holds your whole body."

"Not so," he went on, his eyes drinking in the beauty of his daughter. "Our supplies come from the east, from Pakistan. Khost is their headquarters in this area. If it is not destroyed, we are lost."

"I sometimes think we are lost anyway," she said, her voice a whisper.

"The impatience of the young," Haami said, looking at her with love.

A tall young man, barrel-chested, his features strong and partially covered by a dark beard, came down the path and sat next to Odah.

Salman Amin was the only surviving son of Haami's best friend. Together the older men were the glue that held the *Mujaheddin* as one unit. Together they were the force, the leadership that attracted the deserters. It was for them that the caravans pushed ahead. Hundreds of millions of dollars for arms were donated the world over, but only a fraction of it ended up where the fighting made a difference. Of all the rebel leaders, they alone worked with empty pockets, without Swiss bank accounts, but with full hearts. Every dollar they received went into arms. If every dollar raised were under their control, their small army would be out of the hills and taking back their capital city.

Jalaludin Haami and Hafi Amin believed in one inviolate goal: in the end, not one Soviet would be left on Afghan soil.

"What have you been doing?" Haami asked mechanically. He liked young Amin. He could see a lot of the young man's father in his attitude. Indeed, he looked a lot like his father. His men respected him. It was not impossible that he could be one of the leaders himself one day. His only flaw was his dour outlook and his occasional indecision.

Odah was different. She was bright and quick. Maybe too bright for a woman. It would always give her trouble, this insistence on being one of the men, competing with them, sometimes besting them. She was an excellent strategist. Often he'd taken her advice but in a way that kept her in the background. It wouldn't sit right with the men if they knew they were under her orders, that some of the master plans had come from her.

It was different with her platoon. They had fought alongside her. They had seen firsthand what she could do. They might fantasize about the curve of her hip and the beauty of her face when they curled up in their blankets, but they treated her like a man the rest of the time.

One thought gave Haami nightmares. If Odah were hurt. Or worse, if she were captured, he didn't know what he would do. The self-torture had been as bad as losing his sons. And that had been as bad as he thought it could get. But if she ever ended up in the hands of those savages, the brutes from the north, the *Kawajah*, he would be a man bereft of soul.

Salman Amin's answer brought Haami out of his momentary woolgathering. "Checking on our caches through the hills. We covered the whole southern sector," he said proudly.

Haami knew it was necessary, but it was the kind of work he likened to children's games. In many ways war was like a child's game. *"I'm the bad guy and you're dead. Let's go out and check on the cache in the southern sector."* The shallow approach was a flaw in Salman. He had to mature and do it quickly if he were ever to lead.

Haami knew the boy's father ranged far beyond children's games. Like him, his friend Hafi Amin was dedicated to the freedom of his people. If it took the rest of their lives, if they never saw anything but war until their last breath, they would fight on. That was the way they were, and no item or plan that it took to get them there would resemble a child's game.

"Checking is good," he told the proud young man. "You can never be too sure. It might save our lives one day."

His mind was at work on another thought while he spoke. *This young stud wants my Odah*, he thought. *He's a good boy, but she's too quick for him. It would be a disastrous marriage. Thanks to Allah, bless His name, she knows it, plays him on a string, keeps him at a distance.*

As the thought occurred, another joined them. Hafi Amin was as tall as his son, but thin as a desert tree in a drought, weathered, his brown skin like old parchment. At sixty-three he was five years older than Haami. Despite the difference in years, there was a startling resemblance between father and son.

Amin, too, wore the loose shirt and pants of the rebel soldier, the turban of the proud Pashtun coiled expertly on his head. He wore a full beard, neatly trimmed, unlike his friend's. His eyes were as black, shining with a vitality beyond his years, penetrating, full of question and authority.

The older Amin claimed to be of pure Pashtun blood, the tribe that formed Afghanistan as they knew it before the Soviets had come. Of course, he exaggerated. It was not possible to have pure Pashtun blood, not when they had occupied these lands for more than two hundred years.

Haami knew he was a mixture of Pashtun and Hazarara. His features showed none of the Hazararas' Mongolian origin, but he knew it was in his blood. The Oriental eye came out in Odah to some degree. It was part of her exotic beauty, inherited from her mother, a woman more Hazarara than Pashtun.

"Go with God," Hafi Amin greeted them.

"And may God be with you," the seated warriors replied.

"What is new at the front?" Haami asked as Ahmed Shah crept closer to the fire.

"Our artillery has scored beautifully," Hafi Amin replied. "But it is always the same. Their gunships take a heavy toll.

We managed to shoot down only one."

"We should get our captured gunships in the air," Salman suggested.

"And who would fly them?" his father asked.

"The men who brought them over to us, of course," he said.

"Salman," Odah explained patiently, "we put deserters in the line because they are surrounded by our volunteers. If they turn and run, we shoot them. What happens if the MI-24 pilot turns and runs? He could fire on our people."

"So put one of us in the cockpit with him," the young man said, undaunted.

"Fine," Odah said. "I volunteer you."

"Enough," Haami said. "Conjecture is unprofitable. What do we know that we didn't know yesterday?"

"A new man has arrived from Moscow," Ahmed Shah said. "He is a special representative of their First Minister. A colonel, apparently close to the head man. My people think he has brought a new stratagem."

"What stratagem?" Haami asked.

"We don't know. Not yet. But we will find out," he promised. "Most of what I hear is conjecture."

"Are we having any luck coming up with Russian uniforms in good condition?" Hafi Amin asked.

"Most are shredded or burned. Some have bloodstains that are difficult to remove. We have about twenty, perhaps thirty we can use," Haami said.

"Not good enough. I'd like about a hundred so we can go out in strength. What about Russian weapons?" he asked.

"More than we can use," Haami replied. "You can pick them up at any battlefield."

"I've heard a rumor from some people I know in town," Odah said.

Haami fumed. "I've expressly told you to keep out of the intelligence field," he said. "I don't want you going anywhere near Kabul."

"I'm not leaving camp," she protested. "Am I to close my ears to news that will help?"

"No. Go on," Haami said, knowing he was going to lose most of his battles with her.

"This sounds serious. It's a stratagem that could win the war for them," she said.

"Well, get on with it, girl. What's so important?" Haami said, his impatience showing.

"I've heard they plan to kidnap you two," she said, her words indistinct, her mouth dry. "You are the only leaders all our people will follow. It would be a disaster."

"Nonsense," Haami said. Hafi Amin didn't respond. He chuckled, showing his disbelief by his attitude.

"You should have guards," Salman Amin said. "My squad would be happy to take on the job."

"I think he's right. Salman's squad should be close to you at all times," Odah said. "Also, you should never be together unless absolutely necessary. Make it more difficult for them."

"Enough!" Hafi Amin finally cut in. "This is ridiculous! We must see each other constantly. Besides, I will not relinquish the pleasure."

Haami smiled one of his rare smiles. He, too, loved his friend. But he was a man used to compromise. "Let Salman's people guard us but only on a voluntary basis," he said. Given the choice, he knew the men would prefer to be in battle.

"Well, I don't like it," Amin protested. "I'm not spending my time with a squad of louts picking their noses and hawking around me all day. Forget it."

Salman started to protest, but Ahmed Shah beat him to it. "My intelligence picked up a rumor similar to Odah's, but I ignored it, thought it was disinformation. Now I'm sorry I did. I agree with Odah. If we were to lose you two, it would be all over for us."

SIX

Khawaja Rawash Airport was awash with sunlight. As Carter stepped from the Ariana Afghan Airlines L-15, he felt the chill of the Afghan winter. He was prepared. Before he'd caught the shuttle from Stockholm to Copenhagen he'd bought a sheepskin coat and a few turtleneck sweaters. Back in the hill country he'd wear native garb, but until then he'd be as comfortable as Sven Lundqvist, a Swedish consultant to Afghan Power and Light.

He passed through customs and immigration without difficulty. The officials were all Afghan. Their Russian masters were everywhere. A show of strength was nowhere more important than at the point of entry. Carter's cover was shaky, but it was the best he could do on short notice.

The building was under repair. Scaffolding crisscrossed most of the exterior walls. The part that had been fixed was a sickly yellow stucco. The old part was pockmarked with shell holes and the smaller gouges made by small-arms fire. All the buildings he could see were in the same condition, but no one had money to repair them. The ones beyond the airport that were piles of rubble had once been mosques and hospitals, the minarets broken and left on the debris, the signs designating what had been hospital and school buildings still leaning

49

loosely against piles of broken cement blocks. Carter had
heard that the Soviets had ground down the population's
resistance by destroying all their institutions. Apparently they
also left the ruins as grim reminders of the power of the
invaders.

Outside the airport, small yellow taxis vied for the fares of
affluent Western and Oriental technicians, their best source of
income. The drivers, mostly small men in dirty robes, a rabble
not fit for the army, blocked the entrance and pulled pieces of
baggage from the hands of incoming passengers. They depos-
ited the cases in their cabs, then stood by with the door held
open and a triumphant grin on their faces.

A particularly grubby specimen had Carter by the elbow,
trying to guide him to his equally grubby car.

"No! Leave me alone!" Carter shouted at the man. "No! No!
Go away!" He could have shaken the small man loose, but he
didn't want to cause an incident.

The taxi driver continued to hold on to Carter's coat,
begging him in Pashto, the official language of Afghanistan,
to take his cab. He kept it up until they were free of the others,
then he whispered, in English, "For chrissakes, Carter, get the
hell in my cab."

The Killmaster didn't hesitate. As he handed over his small
bag and stooped to get in the cab, he tried to stifle a laugh.

"I'm Tom Petit," the scruffy-looking man said as he pulled
into traffic. "Operations sent me ahead with your papers and
everything you'll need."

"You've got my weapons?" Carter asked.

The driver passed over Carter's well-traveled radio/cas-
sette deck. His three weapons would be concealed in it.

"This was brought in by courier," the thin man said. "I've
got everything else you'll need at my place."

"Your place? How long have you been here?"

"Hawk sent me in last week. We had an earlier tip about the
Popolov plot, so he gambled, wanted to give whoever he sent
in a flying start."

The small cab sped through traffic. Carter held back,

waiting for more information.

"Howard put together some great stuff," Petit said as he wheeled the taxi between two huge Mercedes trucks. "I've never seen anything like it. He had a very special colonel's uniform made up for you. It's got campaign ribbons, Kremlin insignia, everything. You're the special envoy from the First Minister himself. Got the papers to back up the act. That Schmidt guy's really something, ain't he?" The accent was pure, tough-guy New York.

"What do we have for transport?" Carter asked in Russian.

"An old Mercedes 300SE. Best I could do," Petit answered in perfect Russian. "Had to ship it in special in your name, your new name."

"That the best you could do for a representative of the First Minister?" Carter asked in Pashto.

"This is not Saudi Arabia, effendi. You take what you can get here. Why not sit back and let me do my job?" the tall, skinny man replied in perfect peninsula Arabic, a distinct improvement over his gutter Afghan.

"What's with the Brooklyn accent?" Carter asked.

"Got to keep me 'and in, guv," Petit said in a perfect imitation of a Cockney. "Languages are my specialty," he went on in perfect Oxbridge English. "I'm not great at the rough stuff. You're the great Killmaster. That's your department. My other specialty is requisitions. I find things that aren't lost. I transport things from one place to another."

"I don't want to know the details." Carter chuckled as he stepped from the cab. "Come one. Let's see what you have."

The safe house Petit had established was a small cement-block villa that had suffered in the street-to-street fighting. Again he'd used the magic name, the First Minister's aide, to get the previous tenant evicted. It was sparsely furnished. In the largest bedroom a huge trunk sat in the middle of the room.

Petit opened the trunk and pulled out a greatcoat. It was the best-tailored, most expensive piece of military clothing Carter had ever seen. The uniform was equally magnificent. The special insignia of the First Minister's guard shone from each lapel. Campaign ribbons covered the left breast.

"Exactly who am I?" Carter asked.

"Colonel Vladimir Nikolskiy, special aide to the First Minister," Petit said, grinning. "Here are your papers."

Carter looked them over. "Could work. Who's in charge?"

"General Lorkh. Alexandr Georgiyevich Lorkh, a Ukrainian. He's been here three years, had it up to his oversize rump with this place."

"How does he react to VIP visitors?"

"You should get the welcome mat. He's in big trouble back home and will do anything just to keep his skin," Petit replied.

"That could be true," Carter said. "The Soviets have a bad habit of shooting generals who have failed. Blackmail could be a useful tool for me."

"Your real problem will be a cat by the name of Andrei Obukhov, a colonel, Lorkh's aide. He's the same rank as you and he'll be on your tail the whole time."

"I'm not going to ask how you know all this so soon," Carter said, changing into the new uniform. "Okay. My job will be to welcome each of the two groups on behalf of the First Minister as they arrive. The story for General Lorkh will be to keep each group, the Spetsnaz and the KGB, from seeing each other. The First Minister has his own reasons. It sounds good, but how am I supposed to be credible? All General Lorkh has to do is make one call to Moscow and I'm out in the cold."

"No sweat," Petit said. "After talking to you, Hawk learned that there really is a special assistant to the First Minister. The real Nikolskiy, he's on special assignment. Very secret. No matter who calls, they get the same answer: 'The colonel is on a special assignment for the First Minister,' " Petit said with a chuckle. "The guy really is close to the top man."

While they talked, a slightly built young man entered from the back of the compound. He was dressed in the uniform of a captain of the Kremlin Guard, the Taman Guards division, the perfect aide to a colonel who operated in the Kremlin most of the time. He stepped forward and saluted smartly. "Captain

Victor Petrovich Gusov reporting, sir," the captain said in Russian.

Carter returned the salute and started to smile, his face blossoming into a broad grin. Finally he broke into a laugh that filled the house. He held out his arms and the captain ran into them, sending his hat flying.

"Marianne! I can hardly believe it!" he said as he pulled from her embrace and held her out in front of him. "The last time I saw you was in Honduras. They'd cut off your hair and you were about to be paraded through town and then shot."

"Don't remind me, Nick," she said with a shudder. "I haven't had long hair since." She ran her fingers through the mannish cut.

"Don't tell me that Hawk let you in on this. Women are restricted here, you know."

"So I'm a man, right? I'm your batman or aide or whatever they call them in the Russian military. Seriously, Hawk thought you'd need a liaison with the rebels, someone who could be in their camp when you're not."

"I can't get over it. Marianne Penny. Maybe this will be a better assignment than I thought," he chuckled.

"You can bet on it," she said, her low, throaty voice sounding like warm honey. Marianne Penny stood about five-eight in her army boots. Brown eyes flecked with gold danced in a pixieish face. Her slim figure was well camouflaged in her army uniform. Carter remembered the long dark hair she'd had in Central America and sighed. But he had to admit she now looked her part. She was a good actress, could move like a young man, and he knew if anyone could pull this off, she was the one to do it.

"We'll talk about your role later," Carter said. "But I don't think your place is in the rebel camps—your cover just wouldn't last. Besides, I want to get the lay of the land first," he added, still grinning at her, pleased that she was in on this with them.

"Is that all for now?" Petit asked. They had forgotten him

in the excitement of their reunion. He and Marianne had obviously shared the house before Carter's arrival.

"No," Carter replied, thinking about the most difficult task and now knowing how he would accomplish it. "I've got to find out what a KGB colonel named Popolov planned here before he was killed in Moscow by one of our agents. Someone here had to be an ally of his and was primed to pull off his stunt, whatever it was. I've got to find out who."

"Good luck. I don't want any part of that," Petit said, reverting back to Brooklynese. He pulled another uniform from the bottom of the trunk and was busy changing.

The room had been transformed. In front of a cracked mirror, two men in uniform stood, one a colonel, the other his driver. Behind them, a young woman tried to hide her femininity in the uniform of a man.

"Where's the car?" Carter asked. "We can't walk out of here like this. Not in this neighborhood."

The house was surrounded by the usual compound wall ten feet high. The two men walked to the back of the house where the old white Mercedes sat in the cool of an Afghan afternoon. Petit opened a huge set of steel doors at the rear of the compound and drove the car out into the quiet street. Carter sat in back. He could observe the passing parade of Afghans, but they could not see him through the dark windows.

At the general's headquarters Carter assumed the haughty air befitting an aide to the First Minister. "You will direct me to the office of General Lorkh," he commanded, his face a mask, giving away nothing.

"I'll call Colonel Obukhov," the receptionist, a young Russian sergeant said nervously.

"Are your ears a problem, Sergeant?" Carter said, his manner threatening. "I want no flunkies. I am the First Minister's direct representative. You will take me to the general immediately."

The shaking youth led the way up one flight of winding stairs and to a gilt set of doors on the second floor. The place was run-down, plaster chips and paint flakes hanging from the walls. Carter guessed it was some government building taken over by the military.

The general's personal secretary, a captain, tried to block them until he checked with the general, but Carter pushed past.

"I tried to stop him . . . " the flustered captain blurted out once they were inside.

Two men sat at an immense table in front of a grimy window. The room was large but almost bare. The Afghans had little to steal, and the Russians had given priority to the import of weapons over luxuries.

"What the hell . . . ?" the general started to say. He was trying to rise, his immense girth getting in the way.

A glass of clear liquid stood on the desk in front of him, adding to the countless white rings that had preceded it. A colonel sat opposite him, probably Obukhov, Carter thought. The younger officer was smartly dressed. No drink was evident in front of him.

"You will—" the colonel started to say as he rose.

"I am Colonel Vladimir Nikolskiy, aide to the First Minister," Carter interrupted, holding back the other man's response with a riding crop held out in front of him. He presented his credentials to the general. He went on, holding the colonel speechless with the leather crop and a look of disdain. "My mission here is very private. It concerns a project designed by the First Minister himself. You will leave us alone, Colonel."

The general nodded.

Obukhov strode from the room, his face crimson. Carter faced the fat general, turned on his most charming smile, and sat. "Is that vodka? My throat has been dry all day."

The general stood like a giant toad and glared at the newcomer. For at least twenty seconds the two men took the measure of the other. Finally the general pulled another glass from a desk drawer and filled it to the brim.

The general sat. Carter downed the glass in the Russian manner, in one swallow.

Lorkh filled the glass again, obvious approval on his face.

"You must excuse my aide," he said. "A man of scrupulous habits."

"A rabbit," Carter said with a sneer. He left the second glass in front of him and leaned forward looking into the bloodshot eyes set back in the mammoth face. "This is your big chance, General. The First Minister, unlike the stories you've no doubt heard, is a forgiving man."

"Forgiving? I have done nothing to . . . " the words trailed off.

"We've both seen generals sent home and shot for defeats less than yours," Carter said haughtily.

He leaned back to let the sentence sink in. He picked up the glass and put it down again as he leaned forward. "Is this room clean?" he asked.

"Clean?" The general looked around, confused. Three years in this godforsaken place, suffering one humiliation after another, had taken its toll. The general wasn't the man he once was.

"Clean. Can we talk confidentially?" Carter asked impatiently.

"Oh, yes. Go ahead. No one will hear, comrade."

Carter crept to the door, yanked it open, and caught Obukhov and the captain sitting next to the open intercom. He returned to the desk, yanked the general's intercom from the wall, and sat down once more. He drank the other glass of vodka in one swallow. "Now we can talk," he told the stunned general.

"You and I have been given a task by the First Minister himself, comrade." He leaned forward again, giving the general no time to think. "Within the next few days two groups of fighting men will arrive. You and I will greet them. We will find suitable campsites for them and lend any assistance they need."

"Who? Who are these groups?" Lorkh asked.

"One will be a group of Spetsnaz sent here under the orders of your commander, Field Marshal Anatole Segorski himself. The other group will be a hand-picked contingent sent under the orders of Mishlin Gregarov himself—his personal guard.

"The KGB chief?" Lorkh said, his voice revealing the fear that the name Gregarov usually produced. "What will these two forces do?"

"We are not to know," Carter said solemnly. "I have made some guesses, but even I do not know. I believe it is some kind of contest the First Minister has set for the men who seek to succeed him."

He waited to let this sink in. "It can only mean honor for you, General. It will probably be your ticket out of this place," he said, his expression grave. "And it might save your neck. It will be our job to get them settled. Then all we have to do is keep them apart and not let one group know the other is here. The First Minister was explicit about that."

"I understand, comrade," the general said. He appeared to be like a kid with a new toy. "Keep them apart. Don't let one know about the other."

"Right."

General Lorkh poured another glass for each of them. "Have you known the First Minister long?" he asked.

Carter's attitude changed. "I'm not at liberty to discuss the First Minister's business," he said coldly.

"Of course not. Foolish of me."

Carter rose to leave. "One thing," he said. "Your colonel. What's his name?"

"Obukhov. What about him?"

"He's more than a rabbit in some ways. He was listening in on your intercom," Carter said. "I don't trust him. Keep him out of this and out of my way. Men like him are stupid, driven by ambition, blinded by jealousies. Men like him call the First Minister's office. They check details out for themselves. Very dangerous."

"I understand, comrade. I'll keep him out of trouble."

"I've seen the First Minister demote men to the ranks for nosing around in his pet projects," Carter said menacingly. "Remember. This could be your ticket home."

Before Carter could leave the building, General Lorkh pounded across the office to his door. Obukhov and the captain were waiting.

"Captain, call Moscow right away and make inquiries about that man. And get my intercom fixed this afternoon."

"What can I do, General?" Obukhov asked.

"Get on his tail. find out where he goes and who he sees. By tonight I want to know everything there is to know about Colonel Vladimir Nikolskiy," the general roared. "No one walks in here and talks to me like that."

As the Mercedes sped from one narrow street to another, Petit watched the rearview mirror every few seconds. "We've got a tail," he finally announced.

Carter didn't turn. "Any idea who it is?"

"Been with us from army headquarters. Just one man in a beat-up old army staff car."

"Let me out after the next corner," Carter ordered. "Don't let him see me. Go one block, turn the corner, and stop. After thirty seconds, take him on the merriest chase he's ever had in Kabul, but don't get close to the compound. Okay?"

"You got it."

At the next corner, Carter opened the door and slid behind a pile of rubble while Petit drove off. He watched the staff car closely as it passed. Colonel Obukhov was behind the wheel.

As he walked along the market street, a man out of place among the rabble who were there to barter, it occurred to him that he might be evaluating Obukhov all wrong. Perhaps he had been sent out by his boss. What if the old man just pretended to be a lush? Or what if he was one but was still very much in control? If that were true, the general could be very dangerous indeed.

SEVEN

Carter followed the upper reaches of the Indus River to Qal eh-yeh Sabir, a town at the junction of the river. Petit, the requisitioner, had provided him with a spirited horse, a cross-breed between an Arabian and the sturdy mountain steeds the Afghans used. It had speed, endurance, and the balance of a mountain goat. He had also provided native garb, a set of dull gray shirt and pants, a turban that Carter had wound expertly, and a warm coat, quilted on the outside and lined with short-haired fur.

He stopped at Qal eh-yeh Sabir for lunch. A roving band of Afghans, made homeless by the devastating carpet bombings of the Russians, insisted he sit at their campfire. Sons of the tribe fed and groomed his horse. Despite the horrors of the invasion that had taken half of their tribe, they were still the most hospitable people on earth. It was a reflection on the Communist doctrine that freedom was always the price.

They spoke of the bombing, the senseless dropping of thousands of bombs indiscriminately, cratering the landscape, killing anyone caught in the holocaust, the rape of the land and their people. They sat around the fire, each with a machine gun on his lap, the women out of sight, the guards posted. They spoke of the struggle and of the two leaders they trusted, Haami and Amin.

Carter spoke of a great victory in the making. He was not free to discuss it but was the courier who would deliver the victory to their leaders.

Petit had given him directions to a valley south of Gardez, a town to the south. As he ate a piece of lamb, probably the last of a precious hoard of food set aside for guests, he was told that the leaders had moved. The valley Petit had mentioned had been bombed and strafed the previous week. The leaders had moved two miles to the east, closer to the Pakistani border.

Carter left as soon as politeness permitted. Two of the most powerful young sons accompanied him on their shaggy mountain ponies. These people were hospitable and trusting, but they were not stupid

It took the rest of the day. The sun had dropped beneath one of the craggy ranges of snow-covered mountains before they found the outpost of the leaders' camp. They were halted, disarmed, and led to the center of camp.

Two men sat at the fire, one in his late fifties, although it was difficult to be sure. The other was about five years older. The younger was small, full-bearded, bright-eyed, alert to the approach of strangers. The other was tall and slim, his facial hair trimmed closer than his friend's. He, too, was alert and vital. Carter knew they had gone through hell for the past few years, and their faces, although bright, were lined by the burdens of leadership. They had lost friends and family. They had escaped death a hundred times. He knew what it was like to be hunted, and to be the hunter. These were kindred spirits.

"Sit at our fire," Jalaludin Haami said, waving an arm. He introduced himself and his friend. "We are told you came in peace and with a plan for a great victory," Haami said, his voice strong, his eyes wary.

"You speak our tongue well, but you are not of us. Who are you?" he went on.

A teaboy brought a steaming pot. Carter accepted the clear sweet tea as a welcome diversion. "I'm not sure you will be pleased with my answer, but I hope you will hear me out. I have a very important job to do here that will benefit us both."

"You are American." A female voice spit out the words with contempt.

She had come up on the fire silently. Carter turned to face her. She stood above him as he squatted with the men. Her hands were on her hips. Her body was clothed in the same baggy clothing as the men, but with the eye of a connoisseur, he knew its form was perfect. Her face was perfection beneath the turban, white, unblemished, beautiful without the aid of makeup. Her almond eyes were as black as the full eyebrows and the tendrils of hair escaping the turban. She was the essence of Near Eastern beauty. But what was she doing here? Carter wondered. This was no place for a woman. Not in an Islamic society.

"Is this true?" Amin asked, his face a mask of displeasure.

"It is true. I was not hiding the fact."

"Your people have not been supportive," Haami said, frowning. "But you are a guest at our fire. We will hear you out."

Haami could not help but notice his daughter's hostility toward the American. "This is my daughter, Odah. She is one of us," he explained awkwardly.

Carter nodded at the woman who continued to glare at him. He sipped his tea, letting a minute slip by. The tension eased.

"Three days ago I was in Russia," he said, allowing the words to ripple over them like cold water.

They sat immobile. It was his story. They would not interrupt.

"A KGB colonel in Moscow has started a plan to have you two kidnapped," he said, indicating the men. "A man who works as I do was killed learning of the plot. I have been sent to make sure the plot does not happen."

Haami snorted and waved an arm at the cooking fires of the thousands of men in the valley below. "They will get by my men?" he scoffed. "One man, an American, is going to stop a plot my men cannot?"

The three laughed at him, the woman more than the men.

"Maybe your men will stop them," Carter said, choosing his words carefully. "It would be another skirmish and of no particular importance. But consider this. What if the attackers were not only killed off but the whole Russian army embarrassed in the process?"

They spent a few minutes thinking about this. Then Odah spoke. "We have no reason to trust the Americans. You sat back and let the Russians invade us. Your Congress still debates the promise of arms you have *not* sent us," she snapped. "You have been useless to us."

"My country cannot come out in the open on his," Carter explained, trying to make his every word and gesture as sincere as he felt. "It would mean a worldwide war, maybe a nuclear war if we intervened directly. We boycotted their Olympic games in 1980. We stopped shipping them food. We have made sure the free world condemns them for the rape of your country."

"Congratulations. It cost you nothing. What about the guns?" she shot back.

"Look at the gun in your lap," Carter said. "Who made it?"

"The Americans, but for profit. You even profit from the money sent to us," she argued.

The old men sat back and listened. If she went too far, they would intervene.

"I cannot give you proof, but we are working in every way we know how to help," he went on persuasively, his voice never raised as was the woman's. "The Saudi money you received was the result of our urging. Half of the money we sent as aide to General Zia of Pakistan is secretly earmarked for you. For now it has to be under a cloak of secrecy."

"The Americans are users. They use people. They don't really care," she said scornfully.

"Did I hear my name being blasphemed?" A voice came out of the darkness that had cloaked them as they talked.

A huge black man, hairless, his face scarred on the left side, came into the firelight and squatted between the two Afghan men.

"I didn't mean . . . " the woman said, obviously embarrassed.

"This man is Ahmed Shah," Haami said, introducing them. "This man is Nick Carter from the United States."

The two Americans nodded.

"Who do you work for?" Shah asked, continuing in Pashto.

"I can't tell you. Not for any of the usual agencies."

"A superspook maybe?" he said, rubbing his chin. "Nick Carter. Somehow the name rings a bell. I was in army intelligence G2 for a couple of years before coming here," Shah went on pensively. "Heard of a superspook some of them called the Killmaster." He sipped at the hot tea placed before him. "Is that you?" he asked.

The others sat in silence. The smell of cooking meat filled the air. Carter could see another fire close by and a large spit turning. He waited for a full minute, weighing the odds. Finally he decided this was one time to reveal himself.

"Yes," he said.

Breaths that had been held in were let go. Something momentous had passed between them and they all knew it.

"I don't usually reveal myself," he went on calmly, "But it is vital you believe me and trust me. It is also important that you let me plan your defense in my own way."

"Why should we?" the woman demanded. "I am not impressed by titles. Especially of men who kill for money. You are serving your government, not us."

"I don't think so," Ahmed Shah cut in. "I've got a feeling about this. The army intelligence people spoke of this man with awe. What have we got to lose?"

"You'd defend him—" Odah started to say.

"Enough, woman!" Haami said. He almost but not quite raised his voice. He obviously didn't want those beyond the fire to hear him admonish his daughter. "Enough," he said calmly.

"We all trust Ahmed Shah," he went on. "We should hear out the American, then decide."

Carter could see again that his best course was to tell the truth. As best he could, he told them about the two forces who would arrive shortly. He told them of his ruse as the First Minister's envoy without going into all the details. He had to sound believable, and some of the work he'd done with General Lorkh was straight out of an Ian Fleming novel.

"I have to get back and welcome the two forces, get to know them, help to set them up in camps near here," he said.

"You'll be helping them," Odah complained, her black eyes flashing.

"It is much better for us to know their strengths and weaknesses," Carter told them. "Later we can scout their camps together from here. We'll discuss our strategy when we have them in place. We will know where they are. They will not know where we are."

A servant bent over Haami's ear.

"Our dinner is ready," the leader announced. "I suggest we leave this topic and eat. We can sleep on it and discuss it again tomorrow."

"I am grateful for your hospitality, but I must return tomorrow," Carter said as he rose with them.

"To go back to your friends the Russians," Odah shot back, nostrils flaring.

"Enough!" Haami barked. "You have said enough to our guest. You will eat with the women tonight. Now leave us."

General Lorkh watched Carter step out of the Mercedes with a worried look on his face. He returned from the window to his desk and poured another vodka. He didn't seem to be able to get through the day without it now.

Carter was an enigma to him. The captain had been put off by the Kremlin. The general had called friends in Moscow and they told him to keep clear of Nikolskiy. That the man had power far beyond the rank he carried. Where had he been for the last two days? Where the hell was the man living in the city? He had set his dogs to snoop around for the answers, but they had come up empty.

He returned to his desk and slowly eased his bulk into the chair. He hated this, the politics. He was a fighting man, a general. And he had been entrusted with the war in Afghanistan and had failed. Failure in the Soviet could mean death. It mattered not that no one else could have done better. When they recalled him it was the end of his life.

Unless. Unless the envoy from the First Minister was genuine and favored him as he had so far. He had to follow that lead.

He watched through rheumy eyes as Carter was shown into the room. He accepted the salute, waved Carter to a chair, and poured a glass of vodka for his visitor.

"I do not take liquor while working," the colonel announced.

"But last time . . . "

"It was a less formal occasion. An officer of the state must not drink on the job. We must set a good example and fight the alcoholism that is such a problem in our country, yes?"

Carter nodded absently as he pulled out his wallet and extracted a piece of paper. He handed it to Lorkh.

The general read and handed it back. "You are authorized by the First Minister to take unusual measures to ensure the success of your mission. What are you trying to tell me?" he asked.

"Colonel Obukhov is a rabbit. He is also as I described, too ambitious and too curious. I want him recalled," Carter said coldly.

"*Recalled* . . . ?" the general sputtered.

"You will be better off without him. I have asked the First Minister's office to have Gregarov appoint another aide for you. Perhaps it will be the Spetsnaz officer he sends. I suggest we treat him with kid gloves. Good policy, don't you agree?"

Lorkh heard the words as if from the end of a long tunnel far away. A Spetsnaz colonel as his new aide? A man trained to kill in every way? The leader of the worst butchers in the world? It was all he could do not to reach for the bottle.

Carter saw that he had accomplished enough for one day. Obukhov would disappear. He had paved the way for the meeting with the Spetsnaz. He sat back in his chair, satisfied.

The door burst open. The general's secretary rush in, saluted, and stood rigid.

"Well? What is it, comrade?" the general asked.

"I have a report that a VIP Tupolov is about to land, sir. It's a troop carrier with the Spetsnaz insignia."

The general's mouth opened and shut.

"Do you have a barracks ready for them, General?" Carter asked.

"No. I—"

"Then I suggest you evacuate one as soon as possible," Carter suggested. "Tell the captain to pass the order. You and I will drive to the airport in my car, get to know the colonel, give him a welcome."

"Your car," the general said, glancing at the bottle longingly.

"And I suggest we break the rule for once," Carter said, needing the general's nerves as steady as possible. "Let's both have a glass before we start. Agreed?"

The Tupolov was painted with camouflage colors. It should have looked ordinary, but somehow it looked impressive. The difference was probably psychological, Carter figured. He knew it contained a few hundred of the best-trained soldiers in the world. The only men who could compare to them were those of the Delta Force in the United States and the U.K.'s Special Air Services.

When the four-engine plane stopped taxiing and the doors opened, the troops performed one of their miracles. They were out of the aircraft and formed up in less than two minutes. Carter knew that if this had been an assault, they would have been out of the plane and giving battle before it rolled to a stop.

They certainly looked like the elite force he had heard of, or a fraction of the force. Under normal circumstances they would be hard to beat. But by the time he had to take them on, the man from AXE knew he'd have a couple of aces up his sleeve.

They were under the control of their officers when a smartly dressed man, tall and muscular, broke from the group, marched smartly to the general, and saluted.

"Colonel Rudzutak reporting, sir," he said. He was taller than on first impression, a good two inches more than Carter. He also had twenty pounds on the Killmaster. If they ever met one-on-one, he'd be a formidable foe. As colonel of the Spetsnaz he was probably one of the five best fighting men in the world.

The general saluted. His hand was steady as he held it out. "Colonel," he said, taking the gloved hand.

"This is Colonel Nikolskiy," he added. "As you can see, he's with the First Minister's office. We will take our direction from him."

The two colonels shook hands, knowing they were instant adversaries.

"I have been ordered by General Gregarov to handle this . . ." Rudzutak started to say.

Carter held up his riding crop, stopping the colonel in mid-sentence. "I am not to direct your efforts, Colonel Rudzutak," he said, an enigmatic smile on his face. They were adversaries, but he had a bone. "I am here as an observer on behalf of the First Minister. I may help in getting you settled and into your advance base, but all planning for your project will be your own."

"Good. That sounds fine to me," the general said. "Now let's get your people fixed up. After a long journey they deserve some vodka. Don't you agree, Colonel?"

The two colonels looked at each other coldly. Rudzutak followed as Carter led the way to the Mercedes. The Killmaster

knew that Rudzutak was not cut from the same cloth as
General Lorkh. He also knew for sure that this was going to be
a tough assignment to pull off. He wasn't going to make any
mistakes or be forced into foolish battles where the odds were
long. He'd been through all that before and it hadn't done
anything for him except add to his scars.

Rudzutak was a formidable foe. The colonel of the KGB
force would be a similar adversary, maybe even more formidable in some ways that Carter didn't want to learn about
firsthand.

EIGHT

The day had been filled with tension. As Carter sat in the back of the limousine on the way back to the villa, he thought about Rudzutak. The man was a human powder keg, someone to avoid. He wondered if he gave the same impression.

Petit stopped outside their villa to open the gate, then drove around to the back. As they entered the villa Carter pulled Petit back into the shadows inside the back door. "Do you smell it?" he asked.

"Smell what?"

"I'm not sure. Something foreign . . . wasn't here when we left."

"I smell it now. Jesus! Someone hasn't washed in a year."

"We've got visitors," Carter whispered.

"Holy Christ! I ain't no fighter," Petit squeaked.

Carter led the way inside, flipping his stiletto into the palm of his hand.

Inside the living room, bare except for two chairs and a frayed carpet, Petit stuck to Carter like glue. They were crossing the room to the front of the villa when two men jumped them, wielding their curved *khanjar* knives.

One of the intruders, smelling like a corral of goats, clung to Carter's back and brought the curved blade of his silver-handled knife to slash at his victim's throat.

Carter bent forward in a lightning move, flinging the man against the wall. He had his stiletto in and out of the man's heart before his assailant hit the floor.

He whirled to see what had happened to Petit. He caught a glimpse of him slashing at his opponent with a huge Bowie knife before another foe came at him.

The third man was more cautious. He circled in the limited space, waving his curved *khanjar* left and right. When he thought Carter was sufficiently impressed he lunged, only to find a blade through his armpit. As he screamed and looked at his opponent in horror, Carter whipped the blade across his throat. He went down like a bundle of rags, his blood spilling out across the floor and over the rug.

Petit had one man down. The man's guts were spilled down his pants as he sat in a corner of the room, in shock, looking at his own disemboweled body.

But the scene was fleeting. Another man came from the back door and tried to attack Carter from the rear. Petit already had a second man to deal with. This time the foul-smelling Afghan had sliced Carter's greatcoat from collar to belt before Hugo came into play. The Killmaster didn't waste time. He slit the man across the middle and left him holding his belly together as he went to help Petit.

The small man was down with an Afghan on top of him. As Carter was about to deal with the man, the blade of Petit's Bowie appeared through the man's ribs, front to back. The man crumpled sideways, dying with a gargled scream his last testimony to life.

Carter pulled his colleague from underneath the body. "I thought you weren't a fighter," he said panting.

"Didn't say I couldn't. Just not my thing," Petit rasped, standing before the bigger man, bloody and shaking.

Carter took the knife from Petit's hand. It was huge, much bigger than the usual Bowie. He shook his head and handed it back. Petit returned it to a long leather sheath strapped to his lower leg.

"Who were they?" Carter asked.

"Independents. Roving bands of them all over the city. They must have been watching this place, seen us in uniform before. They don't attack other Afghans."

"Damn! I didn't come here to kill Afghans," Carter said, looking himself over.

Suddenly the image of Marianne flashed in front of his eyes. He charged through the house, calling her name, but she wasn't in any of the rooms. He found no sign of a struggle.

"Where is she?" he asked Petit.

"She has work of her own to do. She'll be infiltrating the Soviets at lower levels, making sure your cover stands up."

Carter let out a deep breath. He was tremendously relieved that she had not been there when the intruders arrived. Remembering Honduras, he decided Marianne Penny had more lives than a cat. She was good, and he needed her alive.

Then he thought of the work he had yet to do. "You've got your hands full, my friend," he went on. "My coat has to be fixed or replaced. I've got blood on my uniform. This place has to be cleaned up. And you've got five bodies to dispose of."

"Hey! What the hell are you going to be doing?"

"Did you fill the refrigerator as I asked?"

"Sure."

"Then I'm going to cook us a decent meal. Better get busy. Your specialty, remember? Procurement. Let's see you procure us another safe house."

As the Mercedes drifted along dirt roads to Lorkh's headquarters, Carter thought about Rudzutak. He had a premonition that the bigger man and he would clash before this was over, and he wasn't looking forward to the encounter.

Carter had Petit drive him to the Spetsnaz bivouac first. It was early but the men were out in full force, their bodies gleaming as they sweated through morning exercises. Rudzutak was one of them. His big frame gleamed in the morning sun as he moved like a jungle cat through the routine. As he moved, his eyes never left Carter. It was as if he had read Carter's mind and was anticipating the encounter.

Despite the hour, General Lorkh was in his office. He looked tired, so Carter came straight to the point. "The other group could arrive at any time. We've got to get Rudzutak and his people into a temporary camp this morning," he said. "Have you given this any thought?"

"We have an area twenty miles to the east at Serubi. It should be ideal."

"Excellent. Your good work will not go unreported. Now, about the KGB group. We will want them to set up in a different area. Do you have a place west of here?"

"At Pahgman. But it isn't as suitable a setup."

"That's all right," Carter said. "Part of the exercise will be for them to set up their own camp."

"What's the reason for the first camp" the general asked. "Why not just get on with their projects?"

"You've probably had the drill on how they operate, General. They have to know every scrap of information possible before moving in. Scouts will be sent out. Plans have to be made based on their findings. Requisitions for special weapons from their home base may have to be drawn up."

"I see."

"One thing, General. We must either provision them completely as they leave or set up a plan for your men to deliver supplies to them."

"Why? They can come in and get what they want."

"They are not to know the other group is here, remember? What if they bump into each other on provisioning trips?"

"I see. But they could bump into each other on scouting expeditions."

"But that's different," Carter said, grinning wickedly. "That's war, General. That's part of the game."

"I've had my people checking on you, Nikolskiy. Colonels don't show up at my command and take over," the general said, his expression more as it must have been when he first assumed command. "I don't care if you are the First Minister's right-hand man, I won't be patronized. Is that clear?"

Carter knew he had to be careful. The general couldn't have learned that he was not the real Nikolskiy. Be he also knew it was just a question of time before the real Nikolskiy surfaced. "I know what's bothering you, General," he said. "And I don't blame you. Don't be concerned. If the First Minister's plan goes off as planned, you will get full credit, believe me."

Carter sat back and watched the general glow. *Too bad,* he thought. *If it goes as planned, the general will be in more trouble than he can handle.*

The Spetsnaz had been settled into their new camp by the end of the day. Carter was tired. His energy had been drained by the tension of getting Rudzutak and his men out of the way before the other group arrived. He sat in the general's office and accepted a vodka. He drank it down in the Russian fashion and this time he needed it. Strangely, the general didn't look any different, but his energy level was better. He was like a light bulb just before it blew. He had been through hell and was living on the edge, the vodka sustaining him. But it was a false security. A hollow strength. Carter guessed the man was going to crumple before this was over.

Lorkh's secretary stuck his head in the door. "Another sighting, General. A military plane asking clearance."

"How far out are they?" Carter asked.

"I don't know," the captain replied. "The tower said they would land in a half hour."

Petit hadn't been able to replace his slashed greatcoat, but somehow he had found an acceptable trenchcoat in the bazaars and had removed the bloodstains from his uniform. The Mercedes gleamed from a recent wash. Carter and Lorkh rode to the airport, Petit driving. The plane was a duplicate of the Spetsnaz craft, but the exit was totally different. These men were not as gung ho. When the doors opened, they filed out casually and formed up, taking their time.

They had none of the show of the Spetsnaz, but somehow they exuded a different kind of strength. Carter, a fighting man, a man used to living on his wits, could feel it. They had the look. Each man was confident. He was fit. And he was not a part of a fighting machine but an individual, capable of thinking. It would be an interesting challenge. Going up against the two forces wouldn't be easy for the American and his Afghan allies. This would require some special strategy, and Carter already had something in mind.

The leader of the group broke off from his officers and approached the reception committee. He saluted the general casually, almost perfunctorily.

"Colonel Vyacheslav Shulgin, General. Requesting permission to conduct exercises in your command," he said. He was a big man, even bigger than Rudzutak. He had to tip the scales at two hundred and fifty pounds. His brown hair was cropped short. His eyes, green as jade, were defiant, totally confident.

"By whose order?" Lorkh asked.

"My superior, General Mishlin Gregarov. I am here at his order."

"The First Minister approves, Colonel," Carter said.

"This is Colonel Vladimir Nikolskiy, Colonel," Lorkh said, introducing Carter. "His job is not to participate but to observe at the First Minister's request."

Carter and Shulgin looked each other over like two junkyard dogs, their hackles up. Again the rivalry was unspoken but totally present. Shulgin would be a worthy foe. He looked strong and fit. He would have to be to hold down the command he'd been given. All his men, a hundred and eighty by Carter's count, were as fit and as alert. He was KGB. His training had been at bases that taught entirely different techniques than those learned by the Spetsnaz. They were the personal guard for the KGB leader, but they were more than that. They were individuals. It was to Shulgin's credit that he could control such a group. They were trained as individuals, but this time they were expected to work as a team. It would be interesting, Carter thought. Very interesting.

It took only a few minutes to get to headquarters in the Mercedes. The men were shipped to an empty barracks block. They would be trucked out to the camp at Paghman and next day.

General Lorkh's hospitality was unchanged. They were seated only a few seconds when the bottle of vodka was produced and glasses filled.

"What are you really doing here?" Shulgin asked Carter after downing the first glass.

"The KGB is not the only department with plans. You are here at the First Minister's wishes, not your own," Carter said.

"I am here at my chief's direction. The man who planned the operation was a friend of mine," Shulgin said as Lorkh sat quietly, content for the moment to let them talk.

"Of course, Yuri Popolov. 'Was a friend' is the key phrase, I believe. Oh, I know all about Popolov," Carter said. "Probably a lot more than you." He leaned forward, close to the face that looked like a block of stone. "This is the First Minister's show whether you know it or not," he said, raising his voice.

"And exactly what does that mean?" the KGB man asked.

"It means that the First Minister pulls strings and puppets dance. Your General Gregarov is part of the chorus line. No one is immune," Carter warned. "One thing I caution you, Colonel," he went on. "Don't make an issue of this. Gregarov knows of my presence. He expects you to represent him and me to observe. So just do your job and leave the intrigue to your boss."

It was a bluff, as with Rudzutak. Both colonels would check on him; they would be fools if they did not. The real Nikolskiy would not show up right away. Carter was sure of that. But he was uncomfortable with so many inquiries to the Kremlin, and all from the same place. The Soviets were born suspicious. He didn't want someone at the Kremlin asking questions that would lead back to him.

He downed his drink and held out his glass for another. He'd have to wait. Wait and work at the same time. When the two groups were settled in their camps, he would have to check with Haami and Amin, report progress, and firm up his plan.

In the same office, two nights later, General Lorkh sat alone over his bottle. The two groups were settled in their preliminary camps. The enigma, Nikolskiy, was off on some business of his own.

It was time for doubts and self-examination. He had let Nikolskiy take charge in the name of the First Minister. He was tired. The whole Afghan mission had been too much for the shoulders of one man. When he'd arrived here, no colonel, not even one with the First Minister's ear, would have maneuvered him. But that was then, not now. He had lost so much in the past three years. He had seen thousands of letters go out to grieving parents. He had seen mass desertions. Memos and angry calls from Moscow were becoming daily fare. He had seen generals shipped home and shot for less.

Now this. All he needed was two factions in a competition he didn't know anything about roaming his area of command, shooting at who knows what. He had not been allowed to tell his commanders in the field of their presence. Christ! What the hell else could happen to him? His own people could get involved with these two groups and it would be laid at his doorstep. To hell with them. He would at least tell his own commanders to stay clear.

He poured another glass of courage and his backbone stiffened. He'd keep an eye on all three of them, especially Nikolskiy. It was time to take charge.

To the south of the capital, Haami sat alone at the evening fire. The meal had been cleared and the other men had drifted off to assignments or sleep. It was a good time. A time for relaxed thinking.

Odah slipped silently beside him like a wraith out of the darkness. He knew what she wanted. She had railed at him since the man Carter had left. She was a stubborn one, like her mother, never letting go until she got her way or the situation was changed by time and circumstance.

This was too important for her stubborn fantasies. He held up a hand in warning. "I will not listen to the arguments again. It is done," he said.

"The man is permitting foreign forces to maneuver dangerously close to us. I wish I could make you see it. By Allah, he could be one of them," she argued.

"Girl, be silent! I have heard enough," he said, his temper, seldom seen, rising to engulf him. "If you persist, you will be relieved of command. You will be sent back to your mother. That, my headstrong daughter, is my last word."

"You are being blinded by this man, Father. How can I make you see it?"

"That's it! You are relieved of command! I will not have junior officers badgering me about my decisions. You are dismissed, girl."

"But, Father—"

"Guard!" he yelled, totally out of character. "Take this woman and confine her to the women's quarters."

The young woman was not taken to live with the women but was confined to a tent, alone. An hour later, a young man, Odah's second in command, a man in love with her, disregarded all the taboos of their society and slipped into her tent. He sat, cross-legged and silent.

The leader's beautiful daughter spent some time flattering him, preparing him for her orders. It was not difficult. Some men in the camp would walk through fire for her. When he had been with her for a few minutes she came to the point. "Assemble my men as quietly as possible outside the perimeter," she said. "We leave tonight on a special mission. No one is to know."

"It will be as you wish," he said, rising.

"Tell no one, Abdi. It is a secret mission. We will forage for ourselves. Tell the men to bring sleeping rolls and prepare to be gone indefinitely."

NINE

"You can't go to the rebel camp again so soon," Petit said. He sat at the kitchen table finishing his breakfast, dressed in his Russian uniform, expecting a normal day as Carter's chauffeur.

This was a new experience for him, working with the best. Carter followed no pattern. He'd seen him at work on the Afghan intruders. He'd seen and heard him with General Lorkh. His new friend seemed to have no fear. He took too much for granted. Given the same job, Petit knew he would have been more cautious.

"They need my reassurance," Carter told him. "I know how they think. Already some of the leaders' advisors will be trying to talk them out of my plan. If they have ten advisors, they will have ten opinions. I've got to see them again."

"You're the boss. What do you want me to do?"

"Stay out of trouble. We're all set up here. Just take it easy but keep your eyes open. You'll have plenty to do when the plan starts to take shape."

"So what can happen to me? I'm not on the line like you? Christ, when you're not here I'm a slug . . . nothing to do in this damned place. It's empty, boring."

He looked at Carter complacently, expecting anything but

what he got. The AXE agent turned on him, almost in a fury.

"Listen up," he said coldly. "You get bored and you're dead. Got it? You're my most important asset on this job. You've got to be alert all the time. *All the time.*"

"Hey! I got it, okay? You just told me to take it easy."

"I meant stay here and keep out of sight. And don't get complacent on me. Keep looking over your shoulder. I don't want anyone finding this place or you. And they'll try."

"Loud and clear," Petit said as Carter left, dressed in his native garb. "Take care of yourself."

When Carter had gone Petit sat brooding, drinking the sweet tea he'd come to enjoy. Marianne came in the back way taking off her military cap and throwing it on a coat rack by the door.

"You look tired," he said. "What have you been doing?"

"Hawk told me to nose around and find out what I could to support Nick. I've come up with something that will help."

"Like what?"

"I'm not sure you're supposed to know," she said, pouring herself some of the hot tea.

"That's just great. What the hell am I, a gofer? I need to know what's going on."

"Okay, Tom, take it easy," she said, taking a crusty loaf from the kitchen table and tearing off a large hunk. "The whole operation is based on a now dead KGB colonel named Popolov in Moscow setting up a trap for the army to fall into."

"That much I know," Petit said, taking a piece of her bread.

"What Popolov didn't know before he died was his boss's reaction. Gregarov didn't know it was a disinformation plot against his rival, so the KGB chief sent in his own group."

"Get to the point. I know all this," Petit said impatiently.

"Popolov set up something to foul up the works. Nick doesn't know what it is, but I do," she said, gloating.

"What is it?" he asked, excited.

"I don't know all the details, but I have a good idea who is here in place waiting for the signal to go."

"Well? Who is it? What is the plan?" Petit asked.

"That's Nick's job. I've taken it as far as Hawk has authorized. I'm to steer Nick in the right direction and let him find out the who, the what, and the when," she said, smiling enigmatically. "Maybe I'll let him coax it out of me. He may have to offer a bribe and I know exactly what it will be."

Petit sat across from her, his brow glistening with beads of sweat. It was the same old story. The heroes always got the spoils and he did all the support work. He was in the wrong business.

Who was he kidding? He was what he was and he was good at it. To hell with the heroes. He'd get his reward when this was over and she'd be as pretty as Marianne. Well—almost.

The horse was surefooted as Carter rode him hard through the hills around Kabul heading for Qal el-yeh Sabir and the hills around Gardez. It was a long and tiring journey.

From the first hour he saw military encampments. Russians and the Afghan regulars seemed to be segregated, but both were commanded only by Russian officers. He stopped several times to assess their strength. They were well equipped, but that might not mean anything. He knew about the Red Army, the quality of the training, the morale of the men.

Conscription was the rule in the Soviet Union. Every six months more than half a million young men would report for their two-year stint. They would overtax the training outposts throughout the country. They would be bullied and physically abused for the six weeks of training. Anyone of rank, commissioned or noncommissioned, could strike them. They would eat low-grade food and would be required to shave every day but bathe only once a week, even in their less primitive camps. These men had been through the humility of basic training and were thousands of miles from home fighting a war they wanted no part of. So they drank even more than usual and that was close to alcoholism for every man in the army.

The Afghan regulars weren't much better. Few of them wanted any part of fighting their own people. They had joined up to escape the grinding poverty of an undeveloped country with almost no resources. To make it worse, they were the slaves of Russian officers and the cannon fodder who were thrown into the line of fire to save Russian lives. The dissidents among them had been made to march, arm in arm, through rebel mine fields.

None of the khaki-clad men Carter saw from a distance wanted to be anywhere but at home. It was heartening if you were pulling for the rebels. Normally scattered resistance in a conquered country had no chance for success. But here, Carter could see light at the end of the tunnel. The Soviets would never have better troops to send in. The regulars would continue to desert. The rebels would never give in. And after countless defeats, questions were being asked in Moscow.

His observations slowed him down more than he'd planned. Around noon he dismounted, sat, and took the sandwich he'd made at the villa out of his haversack. He sat on a rock looking down on a peaceful valley.

The place was an enigma. Here he could sit and look at the scarred brown rock of the mountains and the valley below, green from recent rains, while around him lives were being lost in a struggle that seemed to have no end.

He thought he heard a noise, a scuffling of feet. He sat, totally immobile, and listened. He heard nothing but the wind and the snorting of his nervous mount.

He heard a breach slide open and the distinct click as it closed. It was less than fifty feet away. Carter started to rise when an explosion shook the earth near him, followed by another, even closer.

He dived for cover, looking around to see if his horse had taken a hit. It had shied at the noise but was still there. Its reins were caught on a thorn bush.

The air around him was alive with sound. A mortar! He could see the barrel sticking out of some scruff, an AGS-17 firing 30mm mini-mortars. He didn't think much of the poorly rated guns, but he had a healthy respect for the fragments of steel from the exploding projectiles they spewed out like rain.

The rounds were coming thicker and faster. A rocket shell hit a rocky shelf not twenty feet from him with all the force of an RPG-7. They were giving him the full treatment. The rocket grenade could take out a tank. This was overkill if he'd ever seen it.

Carter raced for his horse, dragged the reins from the thorn bush, and took off at a gallop, heedless of the outcroppings and potholes he'd avoided all morning.

As he rounded a rocky outcropping, he saw a patrol off to his left at a hundred yards. They were unslinging their submachine guns. Soon the sound of automatic fire broke through the steady pounding of hooves. Streams of bullets came at him. Every second or third round was a tracer, a luminous projectile that helped the marksman follow his pattern. The streams of fire seemed to arc lazily toward him, trying to tug at his clothes and tear at his flesh.

His Luger was in his hand. He had no targets. The horse lunged on through the rough terrain, pounding around corners, hitting staightaways at full speed.

A Russian trooper appeared in front of him, his AK-47 at his shoulder. The tracers arced toward Carter. He snapped off two quick shots and saw the man go down as he flashed past. A grenade launcher sought him out, its 60mm grenades throwing up large clods of hardpan and puffs of dust around him. In the distance he could see the orange plastic banana clips on the Russian grenade launchers.

He ran straight into a patrol. The soldiers scattered, falling to each side of the path, some turning to fire desperately, as if at a fleeting ghost. Some were running, fear eating at their guts, nothing on their minds but putting distance between themselves and the enemy.

The mortars continued to rain near him. One blew a patrol from its concealment. It blew them into thousands of pieces of flesh and soiled khaki, cutting short their tour of duty. The debris, material and human, rained down on Carter and the animal.

Then he was through.

The horse pounded on, its ears laid back, froth flying from its mouth, splattering its rider.

Carter hadn't seen an enemy for ten minutes. The horse was exhausted. He pulled up, dismounted, and led the tired animal along the mountain path for a half hour, trying to put as much distance behind him as he could. He didn't want to be on the trail after dark.

His weary feet almost tripped over a sandaled foot sticking out of the scruff along the path. Carter stopped and tied his horse. He bent to examine the body. It was an Afghan rebel, perhaps one of Haami's men. He was unconscious, badly wounded. One round has passed through a shoulder leaving a hole the size of a child's fist in back. He'd lost a lot of blood.

Carter had a couple of field dressings in his pack. He worked on the man as best he could, hoisted him up onto the horse, and continued to the rebel camp at a walk. He figured they might still make it before dark.

Ten men huddled in a cave a few miles from where Carter rode. They sat around a small fire. The walls of rock hid them well, and tea steamed from mugs just filled. All were silent, looking at the woman who paced back and forth at the cave's entrance.

"Are we to go on like this?" one of the men asked the woman. "We lost five men this morning. What is it we seek?"

Odah turned to look at them, fire in her eyes. "Are you sheep like my father and the old men?" she asked. "They believe the American. I think he has motives of his own. Would you be happier if I was banished to the woman's quarters?" She stopped for a moment, hands on hips, staring them down. "I thought we were united for our cause," she added.

"It is not that we are concerned for ourselves," one of the men said. "We would like to know what is to be gained by a small group running around the mountains alone. This morning we lost Abdi and the others. What else—"

"Wait! Listen!" she hissed, cocking her ear toward the entrance of the cave.

So quickly the rebels weren't able to react, two Russian soldiers entered, their AK-47s spitting fire.

Carter entered the outpost of the rebel camp.

"Stand!" a guard ordered in a thick Tajik dialect.

"It is the American," Carter replied in Pashto. "I have one of your wounded."

Hands reached for the wounded man. The horse was taken to be cared for. Carter was led to the fire of the leaders.

Jalaludin Haami and Hafi Amin sat with only one other man. He was younger than they, and he looked very much like Amin.

"Sit, Mr. Carter," Haami said.

He stroke into the firelight, his clothes splattered with blood and covered with grime.

"What has happened to you?" Haami Amin asked.

"I brought in a wounded man," Carter said. "What is going on? Has there been much action since I left?"

"We were told about the man you saved," Haami said. "We are most grateful." He hesitated a moment as if reluctant to go on. He looked older and very tired. "This is Salman Amin" he finally said, "the son of my old friend."

The young man nodded. The three were solemn, looking at the fire, not chatting as usual.

"We are considering our latest problem," Haami said. "My daughter has left camp with her patrol. She has defied me."

"I'm sorry, Haami. Has this anything to do with my earlier visit?" Carter asked.

"That is not the point," Haami said, tracing a small stick in the sand. "Decisions here are made by the highest authority. I gave my daughter a special status because she proved she could handle it. I was wrong."

"Do not blame yourself, my friend," Hafi Amin said. "It is the will of Allah, bless His name."

"Do you have any idea where she might have gone?" Carter asked Salman.

"Why ask me?" the young man replied bitterly, looking at him in surprise.

"I thought you might have had a special rapport with her," Carter said, remembering her beauty.

"You thought wrong," the young man said. "It was her choice, not mine." He turned from the fire and started to leave.

"Enough," Haami said with a voice that revealed a heavy heart. "My daughter has brought a danger to this camp. We must prepare to leave."

As they rose to break camp, an older man appeared in front of them, tears streaming down his face.

"May Allah curse your daughter, Jalaludin Haami," the stricken man said. "My son Abdi is near death because of her stupidity. What is it that she wants?"

"I know not, my old friend. It is my fault," he said, hesitating, then introducing Carter. "This man brought your son in."

The old warrior came forward and kissed Carter's hand. "May Allah shower His gifts on you, friend. Thank you for my son."

Before Carter could reply, another man came running, breathless, to the fire. "Zaki Abdul has returned," he said, gasping. He is . . . near death. Odah's patrol . . . has been wiped out."

Haami turned to the man, speechless for the moment. "My daughter is dead?" he finally managed to whisper.

"No. Odah is alive. They took her. The Russians have her."

A shocked silence followed the news. Haami groped for the side of the tent and was steadied by Salman.

"I cannot believe that Allah has allowed one of His women to be taken," he moaned. Then he tore at his robes and threw his turban from his head. "It was the stupidity of this old fool," he shouted to the night wind. "She should never have been allowed to leave here. I should have foreseen this."

"You are not to blame," Hafi Amin said, standing by, his friend's retrieved turban in his hands. "I was equally responsible. She always seemed so able. Her advice appeared to be sound. We would have made the same decision again."

Carter intervened when they had finished giving vent to their anger and sorrow. "I will return to Kabul," he said. "She will be held at one of the camps. I will find out which one and go in for her."

"I will be with you," Salman declared.

"As many men as you need," Hafi Amin said.

"No, but I thank you," he replied. "You are brave men, willing to fight for your women . . . to die for them." He knew that blatant flattery was the only way to make them see the real situation and agree. "I am known in Kabul as a Russian. I cannot go in with Afghans. You can surely see that." He hesitated before making an almost impossible promise. "I will bring her back," he said.

"What . . . will they do to her?" Haami asked, not thinking rationally.

Hafi Amin, his shoulders stooped, led his friend away without waiting for an answer. It was not a time for such questions or to conjure up in the mind what the question might provoke. It was enough to know they had her.

TEN

He had punished the horse to get back. Odah was in the hands of men who had not seen their own women for months, perhaps years. For conscripts, leave during their two-year stint was not a fact of life. Fraternization was not permitted, especially since AIDS had reared its ugly head.

Kabul was bright but cool the day Carter arrived from the hills around Gardez. The streets of small shops were filled with locals waving hands and shouting at merchants. Tanks sat at some intersections, huge monoliths of steel, as out of place as if they'd been at the North Pole. They were ignored. They served no purpose except as a reminder of the subjugation of a nation, a travesty of massive firepower over the mortality of unarmed flesh and blood.

Carter was reminded of Kabul in past times. The walks through peaceful streets, women flirting from behind thick veils, their eyes skilled in the process, their hands painted to attract attention where faces could not. Men had smiled then. They had been fierce and proud, often carrying weapons, the tribal battles between themselves the only firing that was heard throughout the land.

The Mercedes moved slowly, parting the market crowds, a ship plowing the waters. Through the dark glass, hatred

89

penetrated like acid through paper. Inside was one of the
leaders, one to be reviled, a slavemaster. Carter sat in the
uniform of the First Minister's envoy. But he thought of the
stupidity of ideology. It was not often Carter had time to
philosophize, and he surprised himself that he could now, with
Odah on his mind. But the looks he was receiving, hatred
washing over him in waves, made him wonder why the
Soviets persisted. They didn't need the land. The country had
no resources worth stealing. But it was a gateway to more
conquests . . . always more.

Petit steered expertly through the crowds and to the old
government building that housed the general staff. General
Lorkh hadn't left the building in days, not since the two
colonels had arrived. He had living quarters set up for himself
and made the crumbling ruin a self-imposed prison. It was a
form of insanity, the pressures, the self-flagellation a mental
exercise carried out with shorted circuits and weakened bat-
teries.

"Comrade General," Carter said as he walked in, an authority figure. "I have inspected the camps. It is time they moved
into position."

"My people did not report your presence," the general said.
"Where were you?"

"Your people, General? I saw no people."

"I asked you a question, Colonel. I get daily reports. They
didn't include you. Where were you?"

"I've been scouting the camps and the rebel positions."

The general squared his shoulders. For the first time he
looked formidable. "You are going to tell me the whole story,
Colonel. This is my command and I will not be kept in the
dark."

Carter knew that he had taken the bluff as far as it would go.
The truth, or part of it, would serve his purpose better now. He
told the general of the competition between Segorski and the
KGB director and the task of kidnapping the rebel chiefs. "So
you can see why I'm keeping them apart," he concluded.

"Then you are a kind of referee to see that each side receives the same advantage."

"I didn't say that. Has it not occurred to you that the First Minister may have a favorite?"

"Of course. He would favor one man over the other. It has always been so," he said. "You are to intervene."

"I did not say so. You came to the conclusion by yourself."

"Yes. I did, didn't I. Which one will it be, Nikolskiy? Which one will fail?"

"One is already starting to make mistakes. The fool has taken a woman captive. Doesn't he understand the customs here? The act will put fire in the Afghan's blood. I've heard she is a daughter of a tribal chief. Damned idiot!" he said, getting up and pacing the office for effect. "They will come out of the hills in thousands and we'll lose some of our proud young men."

"But isn't that the objective? Rudzutak's probably using her for exactly that purpose," the older man said, puzzled.

So it was Rudzutak, the Spetsnaz chief, Carter mused. His camp would be the toughest to crack. "But that was not his assignment," he said aloud. "He hasn't the force to withstand a major assault. Your men will take the brunt of it."

"What do you plan to do?" the general asked.

"Intervene, as my chief has asked," Carter said, slashing his crop against a thigh, playing the role to the hilt. "He was most emphatic on the point. And he expressly told me to solicit your cooperation. The First Minister doesn't forget friends."

Carter left the general knowing it would be the last time. He had stretched credibility too far as it was. The next time he tried to play the game could be the last. Right now he had other concerns.

The Spetsnaz had Odah. Why did it have to be them?

The camp was between Paghman to the west and the capital city. They had chosen a plateau, a flattening of one of the high hills. It was surrounded by lowlands, barren hardpan surrounded by towering buttes, sentinels poking their heads to the sky.

Visibility stretched for miles. A man on guard duty could stand at the only road leading to the camp and see for vast distances. Contrails of dust announced every arrival.

Carter stood on a distant hill with the sun behind him. He scanned the camp and its one approach through powerful glasses. He was dressed all in black. Only his feet were not covered in black. The only climbing boots Petit could find were brown, but he had used black polish on them and dulled the leather. Petit had located everything else Carter would need.

The camp was remarkably complete in the few days they'd had to erect it. They'd trucked in prefab barracks, a mess hall, and a headquarters building. The hammer and sickle flew on a flagpole next to the one flying the Spetsnaz insignia.

This would be one of the most dangerous encampments Carter had ever penetrated. Each soldier on that hilltop would be armed with a Kalashnikov light automatic rifle and three hundred rounds of ammunition, a bayonet that doubled as a saw and wire cutter, a P6 pistol with silencer, six hand grenades, and a hand grenade launcher. They also carried a knife that silently propelled a lethal blade as far as thirty feet at the touch of a button. He had to assume they were all fully equipped at all times. This was a forward station in enemy country, an advance training base.

And there were almost two hundred of them.

Waiting for dark, he spent most of the time mulling over strategy. He was left with few choices. He had to get in, find the woman, kill anyone who got in his way, and get out. He didn't have transportation. And everyone he saw on the hilltop would be one of the most skilled killers in the world. He would have to be fast and, more than ever, he would have to be ruthless.

He had his weapons in place. For once they seemed inadequate when he thought of the task he faced. He'd have to use his ingenuity. He'd have to use what came to hand, their clothes, weapons, and vehicles, whatever it took.

He waited through the sun's descent, keeping an eye on the camp, noting the location of stores and equipment. He looked for any sign of Odah. The only place she might be was in a small building with four posted sentries. As he pondered, the sun disappeared, to be replaced by a gray-brown landscape and finally darkness, illuminated only by the stars.

He would have given anything for clouds, but this was a dry season and starlight was common.

He moved down the back of the hill he'd occupied and chose the most roundabout route to the other side of the camp. One side of their camp was darker than the others, but it was also the steepest. He had not been seen. At least no alarms had been sounded. If he had been seen, they were waiting quietly, a deadly horde of trained killers.

The hill was treacherous. The worst hazard was loosing rocks to tumble down behind him and give away his position. He had to go slowly, watching every rock and pebble, moving upward a few inches at a time. It was hard going. Though he was superbly conditioned, his muscles screamed out for relief. He started at nine o'clock and didn't reach the crest until almost midnight.

He poked his head over the crest. His forehead was blackened. His hair was dark. He had Hugo in his right hand.

Few of the men were about. Most would have been worked to exhaustion and would have gone to bed at ten or earlier.

Sentries still guarded one hut, and Carter decided the woman must be there. He hated to contemplate what they might have done to her.

One of the men on guard was leaving his post, moving in his direction. Carter flattened himself on the ground near a barracks building and waited.

The man came on. He was fully armed. The weapons he carried were awesome. He held his automatic rifle in front with two hands, fully awake, alert, ready for anything.

Carter couldn't afford any noise. He slipped behind the man, snaked an arm around his neck, and brought the stiletto

around in an arc until it penetrated the man's heart. The
uniform had to be kept clean. It might be his ticket out of there.

The soldier resisted, but Carter held him in an iron grip. It
took no more than three seconds.

Carter took the man's uniform, wiped the blood from his
knife and the black from his face, and set off, armed as the
guard had been. He didn't head for the small shack immediately. He had to know the setup of the whole camp.

The trucks were all big and cumbersome. They were parked
together at the farthest point from the one road down the hill.
Carter saw two staff cars and decided on one of them. He was
about to set it up for a quick hot-wire job when he saw a small
four-wheel-drive vehicle like a Jeep. That was it. He'd have
some hard going to reach the rebel camp, and the rugged
vehicle would do the job.

Then he saw another vehicle. It was covered with red dust,
almost indiscernible at the back of all the trucks, but he knew
it right away. He'd taken a cross-country vacation on one, or
tried to before Hawk caught up with him.

The words BIG RED could be seen on one side of the gas tank
under the dust. BIG RED, a 750cc Honda that would take him
anywhere. It would be faster than any other vehicle in this
terrain. Using it would depend on Odah's condition. If she
could hang on, no one would catch them.

He checked the gas tank. It was full. The ignition could
easily be bypassed. He started to roll it out from behind the
trucks.

"Where are you taking her, comrade?" a voice behind him
asked.

Carter turned. The man was on top of him, a big man, three
inches taller than Carter. His face was screwed up in a scowl.
But he was not all brawn. He recognized Carter as an enemy
and came at him with his bayonet.

It was a wicked-looking weapon, particularly up close.
Carter had been pushing the vehicle, bent over, off guard. He
flicked Hugo into his palm and waited.

The huge man screamed a battle cry as he lunged. The

bayonet's point nicked Carter as it passed. Carter's hand came up, planting Hugo's slim blade in the man's heart.

The dead man fell sideways taking Carter with him. The machine fell to the dirt, making a hell of a racket. Carter withdrew his knife and waited. A blade whistled past his head and chunked into the wall behind him. He turned and hurled his stiletto. It caught another Spetsnaz in the throat. He went down, grabbing for the blade, drowning in his own blood.

Carter dragged the two men into the shadows and waited. No one came. He looked around the building. The remaining guards still stood at the hut. At least he assumed there were three. He could only see two from his position. The hut was about a hundred feet away. He had to get the bike near it and get close without causing suspicion.

His appearance was much like the guards. They were all in full battle gear. He wondered if they slept like that. The odor of unwashed bodies told him something. They might take off their weapons but not their uniforms.

He got the bike to the back of the headquarters building without being seen. It was less than twenty feet from the guarded shack. Maybe he and Odah would make it. He had a detailed map of the camp layout in his head and knew exactly where the exit road was in relation to the bike. But they would have to run a gauntlet. They had guards to contend with on the way out and everyone else who rose in time to get them in their sights.

He walked to the small shack boldly. He took up the position of the fourth guard. When the others shifted their posts to accommodate him, he was alone on one side of the shack with one guard. Maybe he could take them one at a time. . . .

The guard near him turned slightly, a puzzled frown on his face. Before he could speak the obvious question, Carter used the projectile knife. When he triggered it, he was surprised at its power. It flew from its scabbard to the man's throat so fast he didn't see it. He had to move fast to catch the man before he hit the ground.

The second man would be easy, but he would be within sight of the last man. Carter fingered the trigger of the projectile knife of the man he'd just killed and held Hugo just up his sleeve, ready for instant use.

Slowly he rounded the corner of the shack. One guard turned. The projectile knife was in his throat before he could react. The last guard turned and swung his bayonet in an underhand thrust.

Carter caught the second guard before he hit the ground, turning him into the path of the bayonet. He skewered the on rushing guard on Hugo's needlelike blade as the man's bayonet grated against bone.

Time was his enemy now. He couldn't wait for anything. Odah was inside. She was staked out on the dirt floor, fully clothed, her turban gone, her long black hair streaming out around her beautiful face.

Carter pulled up the stakes and scooped her into his arms.

Her dark eyes flashed at him, defiant at first, then she recognized him. She didn't smile, but composed herself for action. The slightest nod confirmed her understanding.

"I can walk," she whispered.

Without speaking he eased her down and peeked out the door. He needed a diversion. As they headed out, he unclipped a grenade, pulled the pin with his teeth, and tossed it over his shoulder. The concussion from the blast helped propel them the last few feet to the bike. It blew the shack to splinters and started a fire.

"Get on the back!" he shouted.

He completed the hot-wiring in seconds and the motor roared. As he put her in gear the men heading for the shack spotted him. He had another grenade ready to toss. The blast got almost all of them, and the Killmaster rolled the heavy bike over their mutilated bodies and the crater on the way to the road.

Amid the glare of the fire and the acrid smell of blood and burning flesh, it took less than ten seconds to get to the top of the road. He had the pin pulled on another grenade, the spring clip between his fingers and the handlebars.

A guard appeared in front of them in their headlong rush. Carter released the spring and tossed the grenade ahead just as it was about to blow. It took the guard at the knees and blew him backward. The concussion almost tore them from the bike as they passed.

Then they were through, AK-47 slugs whistling past their heads.

The road down was like a roller coaster as they plummeted at a hundred miles an hour. The night took them to its bosom as a rooster tail of dust followed them. Carter wheeled onto the hardpan, away from the dust, and took a circuitous route around some of the towering buttes as he headed south to the tribes and safety.

ELEVEN

In the early morning light Carter lay back, his arms over his head, staring at the roof of the cave, craving a cigarette but content with the progress of the last few hours. He thought about the escape and the gratitude of the woman who, until last night, had hated him. She had been effusive in her thanks, as effusive as an unmarried Muslim woman alone with a man could be. She felt great remorse at her stupidity and the loss of her patrol. He knew that she dreaded facing her father.

As he lay in half sleep, his hands behind his head, the cave darkened. Strange. The light should be even. If anything, Carter thought, it should be increasing as the sun rose higher in the sky.

He turned his head to the mouth of the cave. It was blocked by the silhouette of a figure. As his eyes became accustomed to light and shadow, Carter could see that the figure was armed with a Kalashnikov and the usual three hundred rounds of ammunition clipped to webbing around the waist. A bayonet, a silenced pistol, grenades, and a grenade launcher all hung from the same webbing.

From Carter's position on the floor of the cave, the figure looked immense. He started to rise, but the man unslung the

AK-47 and waved him down.

Carter expected to feel the slugs from the rifle tear at his flesh. He tensed, his gut heaving involuntarily. He moved slowly in front of Odah, but he knew if the AK's rounds tore at him, they would also hit the woman.

Seconds passed. Time for a score of thoughts to fly through his head. He was thinking furiously, but it was no use. He was on his back on the floor, without weapons, facing a loaded gun and a professional killer.

"Get up and come outside," a deep bass voice said in Russian, the words ringing through the cave.

The man stood at the entrance to make sure Carter didn't arm himself, then stood aside as Carter, dressed only in a pair of Spetsnaz pants, preceded him outside the cave.

Carter checked his ground. The area around the cave was flat, free from sharp rocks, but the area extended only a few yards and then dropped off to rocky crevices that would mean instant death. He turned to face the enemy.

Rudzutak.

The Spetsnaz colonel stood at the cave entrance, a mammoth man inches taller than Carter, bigger by a score of pounds, one of the world's top fighting men and one that was armed to the teeth. He could choose any manner of death for his enemy, an enemy who had deceived him, who had entered his camp and killed some of his best men, a man who had humiliated the vaunted Spetsnaz and who had to pay.

He was unbuckling the webbing and dropping it, including all its weapons, behind a rock by the entrance to the cave. He unslung the Kalashnikov, peeled off his shirt, and laid them aside. He was naked to the waist, well muscled, shaped like a wedge.

And he was smiling.

"I'm going to kill you with my bare hands," he said, grinning. "Then I'm going to rape the woman, disembowel her, and throw you both to the buzzards." He assumed a fighting stance. "Say a prayer to the gods you worship, you bastard. These are your last minutes on this earth."

The Killmaster tensed for the battle. He knew he not only had a chance, but it was probably better than even. The arrogant Spetsnaz colonel thought he was invulnerable. He had probably killed and injured dozens of men, taking delight in his superiority, but this time he didn't know who he was dealing with.

Rudzutak advanced in the classic martial arts attack position, one arm slightly extended, one held back, close to his chest, ready for instant attack or defense.

Carter stood erect, holding both elbows out, the palms of his hands forward, exposed to his opponent.

Rudzutak was puzzled by the strange defense, but he attacked.

Carter caught the right-hand thrust with his left, pivoted, kicked Rudzutak behind his ear with his right foot, and, turning, brought his heel down to the colonel's exposed kidney.

Rudzutak moaned and coughed. He leaned forward, heaving bile, finally spitting blood. He was infuriated. He attacked immediately, coming at Carter with a left this time.

Carter had crouched in the unusual "wooden monkey" form, a rare attack taught him by a friend on his last visit to Japan. He was crouched low with both hands like claws in front of his chest.

As Rudzutak came at him, he caught the left-hand attack at the wrist with his own left hand. With lightning speed, he switched to take the wrist with his right hand, placed his left hand on the ground, and sprung, using all the power of both thighs to bring both heels up and into Rudzutak's unguarded ribs under the heart. He could hear the vulnerable bones snap under the assault.

Rudzutak was badly shaken and was still spitting blood. He had probably never been injured in hand-to-hand fighting before. At least three of his ribs were broken, one possibly puncturing a lung.

In the manner of the classic kung fu fighter, Carter was silent. He crouched in a new monkey pose, ready for attack or defense as his enemy searched his confused brain for a new approach.

Rudzutak scowled at Carter's new position. The man from AXE was almost groveling on the hard-packed dirt. As Rudzutak attacked, using a well-placed kick with his right foot, Carter's left foot left the ground with greater speed and countered the kick, spinning the colonel around to expose his back. The Killmaster snapped a crushing hand blow to the other kidney, and as the turn was completed, he rolled to his back, coming up quickly with a flying kick to the right ribs, crushing the other side of Rudzutak's chest, watching without emotion the surprise and pain on the face of his opponent.

Rudzutak swung wildly. He caught Carter a sharp blow to the chin that stunned him momentarily. Confident, the Spetsnaz colonel attacked quickly, but Carter had already assumed the fourth pose of the original monkey kung fu. He was leaning back, feigning an off-balance position when Rudzutak's kick came at him with great speed. He took the kick, absorbing the power as he fell, and rolled, coming up with a kick from the ground that crushed the colonel's knee.

The leg was thirty degrees in the wrong direction. It wouldn't hold the powerful Russian. Rudzutak hobbled sideways to the rock at the entrance to the cave, snarled out his fury, and went for his gun. He had the P6 in his hand was was shouting out his fury before Carter could move. At least fifteen feet separated them. Carter had nowhere to go.

"So it will end with the loser shooting his victor," Carter taunted, waiting for the silenced slugs to tear into him.

"I will shoot you in each kneecap first, then each arm, your thighs, and finally your throat. It will be a fitting death for an American spy," the man said through waves of pain, pain that had made him a madman. Humiliation had taken him beyond reason.

He brought up the gun with deliberation, held it in both

hands, shaking, ready to kill, a wicked grin spreading over his face.

The bark of the gun was loud, the sound hollow. Carter felt no pain. He'd been hit often enough to know you sometimes didn't feel pain at first, but he had not felt the usual shock, the kick that felt like a jolt from a mule.

As he stared at his opponent, half of Rudzutak's skull disintegrated, and as the Russian was spun by the impact, a second shot caught the back of the big man's head. The last thing Carter saw clearly was the hideous mushrooming of the Russian's face, the pressure eradicating his features as the front of his skull bulged forward, blowing away flesh, bone, and blood to splatter the ground around him.

The Spetsnaz colonel fell to his knees, then crashed forward into the dirt.

Carter recognized the bark of his 9mm Luger. From the confines of the cave the sound had been louder and sounded hollow. Odah emerged holding his cherished gun still smoking in both hands.

"He was going to cheat," she said, her voice shaking. "I had him in my sights all the time, but you were doing so well."

She looked at him through eyes moist with excitement. "I feel so strange," she said. "My legs won't hold me. My stomach is molten lead. I have a fire raging that I've never felt before."

She walked toward him dressed only in her loose shirt and pants, the thin fabric outlining her perfect body. She still held the gun in front of her. She walked to him and put her arms around his neck.

Carter felt the cones of her breasts against his bare chest, the warmth of her mouth on his neck, but he knew he could not have her. It was against every concept of decency in the Afghan way of life, of their beliefs since Mohammed walked the earth fourteen hundred years ago.

"I've never felt this before. To see you defeat the brute the way you did. My men fight, but they are boys compared to you," she whispered in his ear. "You must teach me what to do about this feeling."

He kissed her gently on the forehead and pulled her free. "No man alive could refuse you if it was what you truly wanted," he said, looking into those long-lashed dark eyes. "You are beautiful and desirable, but you are Odah, daughter of Jalaludin Haami. I wish that you were not."

She looked into his eyes for a moment, her face expressionless. He expected her to explode, but she smiled sadly and released him.

"You are right," she sighed. "It is sad but it is right, Nick Carter. And I must change my thinking about your character. You are an honorable man."

An honorable man, Carter repeated to himself. He knew that one lonely night in the future when everything looked black and his bed was cold, he would have regrets.

But not now.

Carter took the bloody uniform of the dead man and gave the smaller one to Odah. In the oversized uniforms, they each looked as if they had lost fifty pounds.

At the new rebel camp they were challenged excitedly. It was seldom anyone approached them through the passes of the mountains riding a motorcycle.

Haami approached them silently, a mixture of joy and consternation on his face. Father and daughter did not embrace. It was not done in public. And she had been responsible for the senseless deaths of good young men.

As they disappeared into Haami's tent, Carter was handed a pack of Turkish cigarettes. He flamed one gratefully. The man from AXE found himself the hero of the camp. Word spread quickly that he had entered a Spetsnaz camp, killed some of the men, and rescued the daughter of their most respected leader.

It didn't matter to them that she had disobeyed. She had been brave and taken their fight to the enemy. Only the parents of the lost men grieved and kept their distance. This one, her rescuer, was a man among men, they told each other. He was capable of leading them in battle. They stood around or squatted by the fires, asking questions, prodding him for details.

In Haami's tent the mood was different.

"I want to embrace you, to welcome you back, but I am torn. You defied me, made me look bad in the eyes of my men," he said, his expression fierce. "Your men are all dead and nothing has been accomplished."

"But Father—"

"Don't interrupt. I am not finished," he said, his face sad as he looked at the flesh of his flesh. "What am I to do with you? You are a valuable confidante. You are a competent soldier. I don't want you wasted with the women."

"I have learned a lesson, Father. I will not disgrace you again."

"You cannot have men under your command again. The families would make an outcry," he said sadly, placing his hands on her shoulders.

He drew her to him, pressed her to his thin chest, and pushed her away to look into her eyes. "You will stay with me, close to my side. You will be my advisor. I will keep an eye on you."

"Thank you, Father. I could not stand to be with the women again," she said, holding his hands. "But it would not be right for a grown woman to share her father's tent. I shall have one of my own, keep to myself. It will be a kind of penance."

"As you wish," he said softly. "But you must swear to Allah, bless His name, to obey your father and stay out of trouble."

"I swear that in all things military I will be cautious, a model you will be proud of."

"Now I have other things to take care of. Say hello to your uncle Hafi. Greet the others. It is time I gave thanks to Allah, and thanked our friend Carter property. You were lucky to have a man like him to find you."

"I was lucky, Father. Allah has blessed me with His bounties. I feel like one of the chosen," she said.

"May He continue to show you His bounties," Haami said.

"I shall pray that it will be so, and will work unceasingly for
His continued blessing, Father."

The villa was quiet when Carter moved through the front
doors. "Tom!" he called.

Petit didn't respond, but Marianne ran down the stairs to
greet him. She was dressed in a thin wrapper to counter the
heat. The bedrooms had window air conditioners installed, but
the rest of the house was hot in the daytime. It was late
afternoon. The heat would dissipate soon and an Afghan
winter night would bring temperatures down drastically.

Marianne was not beautiful in the usual sense, but Carter
had forgotten how truly feminine and sexy she was, despite a
boyish figure and a triangular, elfin face. It had been a long
time. Honduras was the last time he'd seen her and they'd both
been too busy trying to stay alive to be close. Before that it was
Singapore and a suite at the Shangri-La Hotel looking out over
the swimming pool and the golf course. The assignment had
bogged down for a day or two, and they'd spent most of the
time in the sun and in bed.

Past thoughts flashed through his mind as he looked at her
standing at the foot of the steps. Her very short hair made her
look like a French gamine of the 1950s, and not at all like a
tomboy. The hazel eyes flashed, cat's eyes, a contrast to the
alabaster skin. Tiny gold hoops dangled from her ears.

She looked good in the cotton robe. Carter was glad he'd
returned to Kabul while it was still hot. He laughed to himself
as he digested the next thought. He realized was was looking
at her like a dirty old man, but he had too many years to go for
that definition. He was still young enough to act, not just think.

"I found a bottle of gin while I was out today," she
announced proudly.

"And just what were you doing today?" he asked. "And

where on earth did you get the gin?"

They moved into the kitchen and she mixed martinis without the vermouth.

"I found a few tiny onions in the market. Okay? We've got Gibsons without vermouth," she said, a laugh in her voice.

"Or we've got straight gin with small onions in it," he countered.

They both downed half their powerful drinks and stood looking at each other, smiling like two kids who had successfully raided the cookie jar.

Carter's eyes focused on the moist lips. The gold-flecked eyes were looking at him openly, intimately. No barriers existed for them.

He sat on the only chair in the almost empty kitchen and looked at her expectantly. She came to him, sat on his lap, and curled the hand holding her drink around his neck.

The kiss was long. It brought sensations from the depths of his being, making it difficult to accommodate her on his lap.

She broke away and looked at him with sparkling eyes. "You remember Singapore?" she asked.

"I was thinking about it when I saw you at the bottom of the stairs."

"Carry me upstairs, Nicky."

The bed in her room was the biggest in the house. He swung her out and down to the soft cover and smothered her mouth with his own. While they kissed he untied the sash at her waist and opened the robe.

He eased back to look at her. She had worn nothing underneath. She was as he remembered, long legs, slim hips, a perfectly flat belly, small round breasts with large nipples. In her Russian army uniform she might pass for a young man, but here, lying on the bed, she was every inch a woman.

Carter tossed his clothes on the one chair in the room and came to her. She held out her arms to him and crushed him against the length of her. She was warm and eager, just as he remembered.

Preliminaries were forgotten. Exploring had been done and

was burned into their memories. She opened up to him and he came to her, slowly as they joined, then faster as she demanded more of him.

The magic had not left them. The moves from crest to crest continued. Unlike Singapore they didn't vary their position. He felt the need to dominate and she was better satisfied with him in control.

An hour passed more like seconds. The sun went down and a cool breeze entered through her window. They lay side by side, savoring the time together, each with private thoughts.

Carter reached for his jacket and his cigarettes. He lit one for each of them. With their heads on the same pillow and the ceiling their only view, they smoked silently absorbed with their thoughts.

"What did you do today?" he asked.

"Spent it at the officers' club like most days."

"But don't they wonder where you get the time?" he asked.

She put out her cigarette and rolled to one elbow so she could look down on him. "I have many faces," she said. "And many voices."

"A pity this wonderful body is wasted in the stiff uniforms of the Russian army."

"Would you have me pose as a whore and get all the information I need while on my back?" she said, laughing.

"No way. I want you all to myself."

She shifted her position so that one breast rested on his chest and her loins were pressed against his hip. "So you could go off with your little Afghan rebel?" she asked.

"That sounds real mean," he said, a laugh in his voice. "I've never touched the girl."

"But she has probably given you the chance. Right?" she asked, her eyes holding his.

He shifted uncomfortably but she stayed with him, skin to skin. " She's an unmarried Muslim woman. There's no way she'd be indiscreet."

"Bull. She gets the itch like most women," Marianne said,

running her hand through the hair of his chest and laying a cheek on his shoulder.

"Scout's honor. I have not touched her and I will not," he said, and wondered why he was explaining this to her. "I'm more concerned about you. I don't like you exposing yourself at the officers' bar so often. Are you having any luck?"

"Not bad. I think I know who the Popolov contact is. I've got it narrowed down to one of three men," she said, raising her head and looking at him seriously.

"That's great. We need the contact. It's absolutely essential. But not at the cost of my favorite female agent."

"Why do you always say 'female agent'? I'm an agent, period."

"I stand corrected, but I thank the Good Lord who made you that you are female."

"Chauvinist pig. I'm just a sex object to you."

"Tell me we've got to stop meeting like this," he said, laughing.

"Pig, I love meeting you like this," she said, sitting up and reaching for her wrapper, "but I don't like this assignment, Nick. It's not Nick Carter. It's more like the Terminator than the Killmaster. Whatever happened to elegant hotels, formal dress, baccarat at Monte Carlo, cocktails at the Ritz, nights at the Shangri-La?"

"I've got to take what I'm given, luv," he said, looking up at her. "Afghanistan is important to us. We cannot allow the Afghan leaders to be kidnapped. Afghanistan would fall and that would leave Pakistan and Iran open to the Soviets.

"But I've come to the same conclusion as you. My cover must be blown for sure. As soon as you and I can get together with Tom, we'll have to plan a whole new strategy."

"Good. I don't like this," she said. "It's not my part I'm worried about. That's okay. I don't like you playing military games. And you're too vulnerable. I'm sure this is not what Hawk had in mind."

"Maybe you're right. I'm about due to call him. I'll tell him we're in the background from now on."

"Wouldn't it be nice if the next time we meet you'd be peeling an elegant gown from me in Paris or Rome instead of a wrapper in a crummy little villa in this hole of a place?"

"Amen," he said. "I'll drink to that. Let's have another of your vermouthless Gibsons or whatever, and we'll see what the evening brings."

TWELVE

Petit returned to the villa to find Nick and Marianne sitting in the kitchen sipping fresh mugs of coffee. He had been out most of the night dressed as an Afghan, listening to the men talk at the coffeehouses, getting the flavor of the war firsthand. He poured a cup of coffee and sat with them.

They looked different. He knew what it was right away. It had to come. The hero had taken his reward. Or was it the other way around? He liked Carter but at that moment resented his own secondary role.

"My cover isn't going to work any longer," Carter said. "We've been talking and we've got to start playing this from a different angle."

Petit was silent for a moment, then asked, "Have you thought it through?"

"Not all the way," Carter said. "Marianne will continue to pose as a Soviet soldier. Her role is less transparent than mine was."

"What's the plan so far?" Petit asked.

Carter unrolled a map and spread it out on the scarred table. He put his coffee mug on one corner to hold it down and put Marianne's on the other. "A town called Soltankhel is the ideal place. I've seen it while going to and from the camp. It's in a

111

defile with a gradual incline on two sides. On this side," he said, pointing to the north, "we have a rocky cliff that can be scaled by agile soldiers."

"Did you have a plan in mind before your Nikolskiy cover was blown?" Marianne asked.

"No point in going into it in detail now. As Nikolskiy I was going to order the two groups to Soltankhel, one on either side of the defile. As myself, I was going to lead the rebels into the defile, draw the two Soviet groups into the action, and then withdraw."

"So what changed your mind?" Petit asked.

"Too many things can go wrong. My cover isn't blown, but I couldn't hope to fool them all the way through the plan," Carter said, taking a Turkish cigarette from a pack and lighting up. "I'm not really a military man—none of us are. And another thing. The rebels should be given the chance to fight their way out of this with our help. It's a matter of face with them. We set it up and they pull if off."

"What about the Popolov angle?" Petit asked. "How does that fit?"

"We don't know exactly what Popolov planned yet. That's part of Marianne's job," Carter said, drawing on the strong Turkish tobacco. "I suspect she'll find out that a tank commander or an air force commander is poised to kill off what he expects is an army detachment."

"Kill off their own?" Petit asked.

"A power struggle in the Kremlin," Carter explained. "A few hundred men mean nothing to them. Stalin killed off millions."

Petit knew he was learning a lesson on the inner workings of Soviet strategy, be he wasn't sure he cared to know. "What was your original plan for the Popolov force?" he asked.

"If I had led the rebels, we would have left the battlefield by stealth and let the Popolov group cut up both Soviet groups."

"And now?" Marianne asked.

"Now, when we know what we are facing from the Popolov

group, we'll give its leader instructions on how to proceed and try to arm the rebels to handle it," Carter said.

"Sounds complicated to me," Petit muttered. "What the hell am I supposed to be doing while this is going on?"

"Same as usual. You might find us a new safe house for starters," Carter said.

"This is Kabul, and it's wartime, remember?" the small man said. "Villas like this are almost impossible to find."

"But you're the scrounger," Carter said, grinning. "So scrounge."

"And what's your new role?" Petit asked.

"An Afghan traitor," Carter said. "A Judas. I'm going to tell each camp how to find the rebel leaders and take them alive. The trap will be Soltankhel."

"Have you decided on the time?" Marianne asked.

"Yes," Carter said. He wrote the date, place, and time on a piece of paper. "This is the time and these are the coordinates for Soltankhel. Memorize the figures."

Marianne Penny took particular pains to dress for the job she had in mind. As Captain Victor Petrovich Gusov, she had to be convincing. While Carter was on one of his trips to the rebels she had work to do.

She donned the cheap cotton underwear of the average Soviet officer and looked at herself in the mirror. Her image in the man's trunks and tank top gave her a laugh at a time when any relief was welcome.

A suit of body armor was hanging from a chair in the bedroom she'd taken for herself. It was a Spartan room except for the bed, which was a huge square affair with a headboard equipped with a host of gadgets including a stereo. It looked out of place in a room that contained only one chair, a dressing table, and a mirror. But she smiled when she thought of what had taken place on it the day before.

Marianne picked up the body armor and zipped it from bottom to top. It was an old model, heavy and bulky, but in fact she wanted the weight and the bulk. With it in place she quickly pulled on a khaki-colored shirt and followed it with a black tie. The effect was much more masculine but it still looked wrong. She'd achieved the bulky torso but above it was a slim neck and small head.

She ignored the face for the time being, pulling on the coarse pants and tunic of her uniform. The socks she used were brown cotton and the shoes heavy black oxfords, steel capped.

The face was still a problem. To detract from her other features she skillfully added a pair of false ears that were oversize. The first thing anyone would notice about the young captain was his ears. No one should have ears so large. She looked as if she could take off and do a few circuits of the area any moment.

Combing her hair in a masculine style altered her looks even more; gone were the delicate wisps that had framed her face earlier. She added dark brown contact lenses, an upper set of false teeth badly in need of dental work, and a few worry lines at her eyes and mouth. Last, she used a special makeup to darken the area that would be masculine beard. The teeth distorted her sexy mouth, the lines added a few years to her appearance, and the overall effect was definitely masculine. Her naturally throaty voice was not a problem. Many men had voices in the same range.

"Petit!" she called.

"Yeah? What do you want?" he yelled up the stairwell.

"I need your help."

She heard him pounding up the steps. She stood back from the door, unsnapped her holster flap, and drew the Makarov pistol.

Petit appeared at the door. He was met by a Soviet army officer pointing a pistol at his gut. He sucked in his breath. "What have you done with the woman?" he asked in Russian, raising his hands away from his sides.

"Nothing," she said, laughing as she holstered the gun. "I needed a test. Looks like I passed."

"Holy shit," Petit breathed. "You scared the hell out of me. I've never seen you in your full Russian getup before. You got it down just right. The ears are what do it. What a pair of wings!"

"So you think I pass?" she said, turning for him to get the full effect.

He examined her and came closer. He sniffed for any lingering signs of her femininity. She smelled of carbolic soap and moth balls.

"You pass," he said, grinning. "And no dame is going to make a pass at you. With those teeth and ears, you're even ugly for a guy."

"Then get into uniform and drive me to the officers' club. I've got to become a constant visitor at their watering hole."

At the villa, Carter strode into the house, dressed as a rebel and streaming the dust of the trail behind him.

"Tom!" he shouted. "Petit! Where the hell are you? I need a clean robe and I've got to get over to Shulgin's headquarters."

He waited but heard no reply. He'd seen the trunk of the Mercedes out back and a flash of yellow that was the small taxi. If Petit was out, he'd have to be on foot, but Carter couldn't remember seeing his helper walk as far as the corner store.

The downstairs was empty. He was about to climb the stairs and find the robe himself when he thought of the kitchen. Maybe Petit couldn't hear him from back there.

"Tom!" he yelled again. "I've got to be on my way."

Inside the kitchen he stopped in his tracks. Tom Petit wasn't about to answer him. He was pinned to the wall with two commando knives, one through each thigh. He was upside down, his throat cut, blood covering his face.

Carter had seen this sort of gruesome execution in Thailand. It had been a favorite trick of a sadistic and totally mad Cambodian colonel. He'd never seen this particular display anywhere else, or as the tactic of a Soviet brigade.

"He died hard. A real fighting cock," a gruff voice said in Russian.

Carter whirled to face the intruder.

Shulgin.

"It was you!" was all he could get out.

"I saw you on the trail, 'Colonel Nikolskiy.' You should have been more careful," Shulgin spat out. "The fabled American Killmaster, right? The little bastard managed to gargle it out before he died."

Carter stood not ten feet from Petit's murderer. The six-foot-six KGB colonel blocked the light. He was armed with every weapon the Spetsnaz carried and he went them one better: he had a rocket launcher strapped to his massive back.

Overkill. He had enough armament to bring down the whole villa.

Carter didn't waste time on niceties. He whipped Hugo into his palm and flipped it in one lightning motion to the man's throat.

Shulgin moved his head as fast as Carter threw. The stiletto chunked into the wood and wavered behind the colonel's head while the giant grinned wickedly.

Carter reached for Wilhelmina only to have the Luger kicked from his hand before he could get off a shot. The giant was fast, as fast an opponent as Carter had ever seen.

While the thought occurred, Shulgin pulled a grenade from his webbing, pulled the pin, and tossed it at Carter's feet. The Killmaster leaped to one side as the grenade exploded. He expected to be wounded by slivers of steel as the fragmentation grenade went off, but he was wrong. It was phosphorous. Hundreds of white-hot blobs of the chemical hit the walls, and the kitchen was an inferno in seconds.

Carter tore off his burning shirt and pants. The Russian had retreated to another room, roaring out his challenge for Carter to come after him.

As Carter rounded the corner, the whole wall mushroomed into a thousand fragments as the rocket launcher whooshed a rocket grenade past him into the wall. His back was peppered with plaster. It was painful but not fatal. He went after the Russian into the next room, not knowing what to expect next.

Only seconds had passed since the fire started, but the whole villa was already threatened. The roof sagged in the middle where the supporting wall had been blown away.

Carter charged the bull of a man. He was caught by Shulgin, lifted off his feet, and flung against a far wall. He struck the wall with the flat of his back, and as he skidded to the floor the wind was knocked from him.

Smoke filled his lungs. He could see spots of white and green flash behind the lids of his eyes. Heat was building within the villa.

The huge KGB officer came after him again. He picked him up, whirled him around, and prepared to toss him into the inferno.

Carter was not quite unconscious. His fingers brushed against a grenade at the giant's waist. He plucked it free, pulled the pin, and stuck it inside the man's shirt.

He was flung through the air, into the middle of the fire. He hit the floor in a roll as a blast shook the villa.

Wilhelmina was on the floor in a corner. Hugo was still sticking in the wall close to the flaming doorframe. He snatched at both. The heat of them almost took the skin from the hands that had been frozen in Leningrad. As he raced for the upper floors, Leningrad seemed so long ago.

The whole house was in flames now. As he passed the front room on his desperate flight to save some of his treasures, he saw the Russian. Shulgin was on his back, almost cut in two by the explosion. His face registered surprise as his hands, red with his own blood, felt through the massive hole seeking the guts that were not there.

Carter didn't break stride. He headed for his bedroom, bundled up the rest of his clothes, and vaulted from the window to a shed roof and to the ground.

He didn't give Shulgin another thought.

Shulgin would fry.

• • •

Marianne entered the mess hall without causing much of a stir at first. She'd changed her insignia. She was with the Inspector General's office, a branch of the army everyone feared. The IG's people came and went as they pleased, sticking their noses in where they weren't wanted, and they weren't wanted anywhere. The marshal heading up the infamous inspection section was ruthless and chose only men who were stamped in his mold.

Marianne walked to the bar and drank alone. Her insignia made her a leper. That was all right with her. She would pick her spots, make her own breaks. She glanced at her watch. Six o'clock.

Three men sat at the far end of the bar from Marianne. They showed an unusual military insignia, one Marianne hadn't seen in the recognition room back at Dupont Circle. They looked like veterans, their faces lined, serious and unfriendly. Marianne sidled over and introduced herself.

With her at their elbow, the three looked uncomfortable. They didn't show fear for her insignia as would most newly commissioned men, but disdain. They'd probably been fouled up by the department she represented at some time during their careers. They gave her plenty of room, exchanging meaningless small talk that could not reflect on them or their outfit.

"Used to know a man in your outfit," Marianne lied. "Yuri Popolov. Great guy," Marianne said, sipping her beer and looking them in the eye, one after the other. "I was told he left you to work for the KGB. Never figured why he'd leave the army to go there."

They exchanged looks, shrugged, and split up. Two eventually drifted away. The third, a major, accepted a drink from Marianne.

"How well did you know Popolov?" the major asked.

"Better than most," Marianne answered casually. "I was supposed to pass along some information here, but he died before he told me the man's name."

"Popolov is dead?" the major said, shocked.

"Killed by some American spy. But Yuri got the bastard. I heard they killed each other. One hell of a battle. Bad. Real bad."

"What information did he give you?" the major asked nervously. He downed his vodka in one gulp and stood awaiting the answer as if it was a matter life and death to him.

"Sorry I brought it up, comrade. It's private. I'm only supposed to tell one man."

After a long silence in which beads of sweat broke out on the major's brow he said, "Suppose I'm the man."

"No problem," Marianne said, slurring her Russian, sounding like a soldier who'd had one too many. "All you've got to do is prove that to me and we're in business. What's your outfit? What did he tell you to do?"

"If he didn't tell you, he didn't want you to know," the man said, his confidence returning.

"What the hell did he tell you about the action?" Marianne asked.

"Popolov didn't want the Spetsnaz to win a certain battle. That's all I know," the major said uncertainly.

"Dangerous stuff to be talking to someone like me about, comrade. Dangerous," Marianne said, laughing.

"Maybe. Maybe not. But you mentioned Popolov, not me," the major said, taking a gulp of the fresh drink the bartender had left, hesitating before going on. "I've been primed for weeks. So when you finally show up . . ."

"I have the information you need, but our friend said nothing about payment," Marianne said. "Rubles I don't have."

"That has been taken care of. No problem," the major said, clapping Marianne on the back for the benefit of prying eyes. "You don't do this kind of favor for rubles."

As expected, the others in the room noted the action and frowned. You didn't suck up to the IG's people.

Marianne hadn't figured out the whole play herself until that moment. Now it came to her as if the thought had been in her brain since birth. But she wasn't about to give everything and get nothing. It was worth another try. "You command a tank corps?" she asked, hoping the major would be proud enough of his outfit to confirm her thinking.

The major laughed, a hearty belly laugh that was genuine. "As far from the truth as possible, comrade."

"What's so funny?"

"You'll never know. Not unless you're there when I pull the plug. Are you going to be there, comrade?"

"My part is to get the Spetsnaz to the right place at the right time. I don't want to get involved in your action, Major," she said, trying to browbeat confirmation out of the man.

"Then you'd better stand clear. Its going to be quite a show," the major said. "That's all you're going to find out."

Marianne knew she'd taken it as far as she could. She'd exposed herself too long as it was. "Okay. I respect Popolov's wishes. Here are the coordinates and the time," she said, whispering the map coordinates and four digits of the twenty-four-hour clock that Carter had given her just hours before.

"What will your play be? I have to know what to strike at," the major said.

"The rebels will be dressed as Afghan regulars right down to their army-issue skivvies," Marianne said, ordering another round. "They and the Spetsnaz will really be into it . . . hand-to-hand fighting. You can't miss it."

"Sure I can. Not easy to spot."

"You bastards always want someone to point the way for you," Marianne jeered. "Okay. I'll have someone in the hills fire a star shell over the action." She downed the drink that had just been brought. She turned to leave, burped, and lurched for the door. "And you bastards keep the hell away from the guy who fires the star shell for you."

She had him. She had all the pieces. Now the problem was to help Nick get the equipment to crush the major and his men. She knew who they were and what they were, and she knew how to stop them. Now all she needed was the birds to do the job.

THIRTEEN

Carter didn't have a lot of choice. Marianne had a radio she could use, but he had nothing. So it was the local public telephone for him. He gave the operator the number in Farsi and when the AXE computer came on line, he continued in Farsi, complaining of a business deal that had gone wrong.

He sweated it out in the phone booth, not knowing if Hawk's experts had programmed the computer for the Iranian language.

"We do not have the information here. We suggest you contact Mr. Petit's local supplier," the computer said, disconnecting before he could say more. This was the ultrasophisticated computer communications system Hawk had installed when he'd had his fit of computer madness a couple of years back. Some software jockey had programmed in a honeyed voice that often enough bugged Carter when he was in a hurry. This time he could have kissed the damned thing. Petit's local supplier? How the hell was he supposed to find the supplier? Of course they wouldn't know that Tom was dead.

Wait a minute. Tom Petit had handed over the Killmaster's weapons in the taxi the first time they met. Carter had shipped

121

them in through a local embassy so often he hadn't given it any thought.

But there was no way they could have an embassy or consulate in a Soviet battle zone. The U.S. hadn't had one since their ambassador was killed back in the late seventies. Damn! Where did Tom pick up his weapons? The computer probably knew but couldn't tell him over the wide-open Afghan telephone system.

He went to a local café and asked for a cup of tea. In the crowded open-air restaurant he willed himself to think, to remember everything Petit had said, even the most inconsequential pieces of information.

Petit had called the place where he'd acquired a lot of material by a special name. Carter thought the name strange at the time, but he'd been preoccupied. Now he racked his brain. What was it?

Carter cursed himself for taking Tom Petit for granted. Then he cursed himself for not being able to remember. When he remembered would it do him any good?

Contact Mr. Petit's local supplier, the computer advised. He left the table and sought the toilet at the rear of the restaurant.

The small room was as filthy as any he'd seen on his travels. The tiled walls were literally black with scum. The conical hole in the floor, the Eastern toilet, was filled with excrement. The floor was covered with water that dripped from the flexible hose that the men used to clean themselves.

Carter was interested in the robe he wore. Petit had provided it as he had all the others. He pulled it over his head and looked for a label, anything that would help.

A small label was ironed to the back of the yoke:

IBRAHIM 7 SMALL EXHIBITION
YOUR LOCAL AGENT—IMPORT, EXPORT,
COMMUNICATIONS

It was of no use to him. The word *communications* didn't fit an import and export firm. The rest of the label meant nothing to him.

Hey. Maybe . . . Bingo! Small . . . *petit*. *Petit* was the French word for small. *Petit* for masculine, *petite* for feminine. Now, where in hell was he to find Ibrahim and Small? The phone book.

He put his full-length native robe back on and returned to the coin telephone he'd used earlier. The book was a shambles. It contained no Ibrahim and Small. It would be a new number. No harm in calling information for it.

The information operator seemed to take forever. Unlike some Middle Eastern countries like Saudi Arabia, Kuwait, and the Emirates, the telephone service was primitive. Finally he dialed the number.

"Ibrahim and Small Exhibition," a voice that sounded young answered in Pashto.

"I'm a friend of Mr. Small," Carter said, choosing his words carefully. "I have a message from him."

"You can give me the message," the voice said, a note of suspicion creeping in. His accent was peculiar and he spoke slowly.

"I must pass it on in person. I am also a partner of Mr. Tom."

"Mr. Tom? You are a partner? Come to Faisal Street in the market. You will see my sign."

"Carter hated blind meetings, but he had little choice. The villa was destroyed. He couldn't hang around the scene waiting for Marianne. The place would be swarming with KGB. He only hoped that Marianne got clear before they spotted her. And he had to set up a meet with her soon so they could plan the next phase. They needed a new safe house. Perhaps Ibrahim could help with that.

He had not paid much attention to signs when in the rabbit warren that was the local market. Souks filled every cobblestone street. Bare bulbs lighted the narrow alleys between the rows of small stores. Overhead, the alleys were covered with rows of rough wooden logs covered with palm fronds and a solid coating of cement like dirt.

Women squatted at every turn in the the crowded streets, their heads and bodies covered in black, their eyes shining through mesh veils.

Men sat in their small booths indifferent to the passing crowd. Some bartered with those who stopped to browse or buy.

One other group were obvious by their presence. KGB military guards paraded in twos, their shouldered Kalashnikovs an obvious threat.

Each small stand had a sign telling the name of the proprietor and his line of goods, although the kind of business in each case was obvious. Rug merchants opened stores close to each other. Merchants selling pots and pans congregated on the same streets.

Carter asked a passing man where the import-export businesses were. The Afghan looked at him questioningly and pointed in the direction Carter had just come.

"Outside. The street next to the mosque."

Great. There was a mosque on almost every corner. But at least he knew it was outside the dark alleys.

The sun hit him like a Hollywood searchlight as he stepped from the gloom. He blinked a few times and waited for his eyes to adjust. When they did, he was staring at the sign: IBRAHIM & SMALL EXHIBITION. It was new, the paint hardly dry.

Marianne cursed Tom Petit silently as she sat in the back seat of the small yellow taxi she'd had to take because he hadn't picked her up as agreed. When the taxi neared her destination the driver stopped in the middle of the street and turned to her.

"We cannot go here, Mr. Officer. Some spy's house was burned here. Two bodies in the ashes," he said, turning toward her, his breath bad enough to kill a grown horse. "Burning is not a good way to journey to the House of Allah, bless His name.

"You want to walk the rest of the way?"

Marianne's blood chilled as she realized what his words meant. They had been blown. Two bodies in the house. Was one of them Tom or Nick? Either way she didn't want to think about it. It could be both of them. They could both be dead. *Nick could be dead.* If he was, she was out in the cold with no time to mourn.

What should she do? she asked herself. She had her briefcase—for the last few days she'd had it with her constantly—so she had her radio. She could get to the AXE network computer.

She realized the Afghan cabbie was waiting for an answer. "Do you know a restaurant where other officers like me would go?" she asked.

"I know, Mr. Officer. I know it in Russian," he said. "You speak our language very well. Not many of you do."

Another slip? Was she getting paranoid? She should stick to Russian all the time. The KGB could have spies everywhere. Like the man said, not many of the occupiers spoke the Afghan language.

"Some of us do. We must so we can govern this miserable piece of real estate," she said curtly. "Now, about that restaurant?"

"The Intercontinental Hotel. I take many there."

A new idea occurred. She had plenty of money and ID. She would take a hotel room and make the call to Hawk from there.

As they drove she said over and over to herself, Please God, please. Let them be alive.

A young Afghan lounged against the door of the store. He wore his turban coiled differently. The upper half of the coils swirled up like a chef's hat.

"I called Mr. Ibrahim. I am also a partner of Mr. Tom," Carter told him. "I would like to talk with Mr. Ibrahim."

The young man walked to the back of the store and stopped behind a huge unopened crate. "I am Mohammed Abdul Azziz Ibrahim. How is it that you are a partner of Mr. Tom?"

"We call our establishment Koshin and Petit," Carter said.

"Your Pashto is better than mine, Mr. Nick Carter," Ibrahim said in English.

Wilhelmina was in Carter's hand in less time than it took Ibrahim to blink. "Just who the hell are you?" he asked.

"Why does an Afghan merchant speak his language so poorly?"

Ibrahim laughed and tried to brush the gun away. Carter grabbed him and held the gun to his neck.

"A poor slob trying to make a buck," Ibrahim managed to say. "My folks are from here. They moved to the States when I was a kid. Hey! I just wanted to help, okay? I moved here after the embassy was cleaned out in '79. I knew enough Pashto to get by."

"Who do you work for?" Carter barked.

"I'm independent. The CIA has almost nothing going for it here. The Brits haven't been able to establish any M16 people. Nobody else cares."

Carter took the Luger from Ibrahim's throat. "How did you connect with Tom Petit?"

"Your people know about me. They used me to get that damned gun in for you."

Carter put the gun away and stepped back a pace or two. "I'm listening," he said.

"I give out my name selectively or I'm dead."

"It figures that my people know about you."

"Your top man knew about me, but your computer figured it out. Tom told me about it. Damned electronic genius took the name from one of Tom's invoices. It matched it with the Afghan telephone records for new service and came up with me. It's electronic logic process made an assumption that was right on the money."

"I wouldn't be so happy about that if I were you. What one computer can do, another might."

"I doubt it," the young Afghan-American said.

"What's with the sign? You couldn't have been in business with Tom very long." They were speaking English now.

"Tom's idea of insurance. Looks like it paid off."

Ibrahim's accent was midwestern. He was frowning. "What did you mean by 'couldn't have been'? Where's Tom?"

"Tom is dead. That's why I'm here," Carter said.

"A bummer. I liked the guy, you know? I'm sorry as hell."

"I understand. I feel badly too. But life goes on. Right now I've got to call my people on a clean line."

Ibrahim led the way to a back room. He opened a cupboard and switched on a powerful radio.

"Do the Soviets triangulate on this?" Carter asked.

"They don't have any equipment in Kabul right now. It's all in the mountains."

"Better mind the store," Carter said, nodding in the direction of the door.

When he was gone, Carter swung the dial to a frequency the AXE computer monitored at all times and gave his call number and a code sequence.

"You found Ibrahim," the computer said.

"Just put me through to Hawk, okay?" he said. He hated dealing with artificial intelligence.

"My, aren't we touchy today," the synthesized electronic voice said.

In less than ten seconds the gruff voice of his mentor answered. He was glad to hear the familiar growl even if the old man sounded annoyed.

"It's Nick. I need to get a message to Marianne," Carter said.

"I take it things aren't going well."

Carter could tell from the slightly slurred enunciation that the familiar cigar was rolling from side to side in Hawk's mouth as he spoke. "Tom bought it today and my cover is blown," he said. "Marianne is all right as far as I know, but she doesn't know that I'm alive or where to meet up with me."

"She hasn't called here yet. What do you want me to tell her?"

"I'll hang out with Ibrahim at Ibrahim and Small." He gave

Hawk directions for the woman. "She can pick me up at Ibrahim's. I'll have a new safe house by the time she finds me."

"Anything we can do at this end?"

"Not yet. We've set the date and time for the final confrontation. We might need some armament. I'll probably have her call Howard."

"You're not getting into this too deep?" Hawk asked. "I don't want you in the middle of a battle."

"I agree. At first it seemed the natural thing to do. But I changed by mind for a couple of reasons."

"One reason is face, right? You have to let the rebels win the battle themselves," Hawk offered.

"That's one. The other is unpredictability. The Afghan rebels agree to a plan and then go off in six different directions when they start to carry it out," Carter said. "I'm not a coward and I'm not a fool. I'm going to set it up for them and watch from a healthy distance."

"You want to talk to anyone else here?" Hawk asked.

"Not now. When Marianne calls in for supplies, tell Howard to include a video camera and a battery pack. I'm going to bring the battle back to you in living color."

A wicked chuckle came across the connection. "You do that, Nick. And be careful. Don't get caught in the cross fire."

After the call Carter went to the front of the store and stood talking to Ibrahim while they watched the crowds drift by. Their conversation could not be heard from five feet away.

"I need a safe house," Carter said.

"I've got the perfect place, but your last one was burned to the ground," Ibrahim complained.

"It won't happen again. I'll be out of here in four days, five at the most."

"The KGB can find you in one day. I can't afford to have this one damaged."

"What is it?"

"A friend's villa. A member of the Afghan diplomatic corps. He's in Europe and I have his keys."

"Diplomatic corps? That's a joke. Where the hell do you make friends like that?"

"A very useful man to know," Ibrahim said, a little smile on his face. "I have many contacts and I don't like many of them. Liking is not a criteria." He handed over a key to the outer gate and one for the house. "It's empty and has no immediate neighbors. Don't make your presence obvious."

"I'll have to hang around here. My partner will be meeting me here."

"Marianne Penny? Some partner."

"Do you know everything that goes on in Kabul?" Carter said with a laugh. He could afford to laugh. An ally like this one was worth his weight in platinum.

"This is business, Carter," Ibrahim said with a straight face. "I'll bill your boss for all of it."

Carter was first out of the taxi. He waited until Marianne was beside him and the taxi out of sight before he opened the huge steel gates and closed them behind them.

The villa was luxurious. Obviously diplomats did very well for themselves despite the war. Four onion-dome towers ranged down each side of the roof. The structure had to be fully two hundred feet square in a compound at least five hundred feet square.

Carter opened the front door to a luxurious foyer. The floors were all marble. The most beautiful carved staircase Carter had ever seen curved gracefully to the upper floor. Marianne started up the stairs while he locked the front door. By the time he joined her she was in the master bedroom scratching her ears, the false ones resting on a dressing table.

The room was huge and ornate. The bed was fully ten feet by eight. The headboard contained an expensive stereo, a VCR, and enough controls for a 747. The room's television was flush mounted in the opposite wall. It had to be at least three feet wide.

They didn't have anything to say in the taxi and the silence continued in the bedroom. Marianne folded the Soviet uniform carefully over a chair and headed for the bathroom in the ridiculous cotton underwear that was part of the uniform.

The bathroom was almost as large as the bedroom. In one corner, recessed in a raised platform reached by five carpeted steps, a bath beckoned. It was large enough for a quartet of bathers. Marianne reached down and twisted the gold faucets. A mist started to form in the room.

Carter followed her in and knew exactly what she was thinking. He felt grubby in the Afghan robe and turban. He slipped the long robe over his head and watched as she pulled off the cotton underwear. He was so glad to see her. She turned to him and slowly unwound his turban, her erect nipples caressing the hair of his chest.

He picked her up. Her lips found his as he carried her to the water that was gushing in at an incredible rate. The tub was half filled already.

The water was hot but not unbearable. Carter eased himself down in one corner of the tub. It was molded to take a body about his size. Marianne squirmed around to lie on top of him, her lips refusing to release his, her tongue starting a wild game inside his mouth.

Carter picked up a bar of scented soap and started to soap the woman who pressed herself to him from toe to forehead. The water reached to the perfect globes of her small bottom. He ran his hands over her sleek thighs, distributing the suds, then ran his hands up the small of her back to the wider area of her shoulders.

Without releasing his mouth she eased away from him enough to permit him to lather her breasts, her stomach, and finally the dark patch of hair at her loins.

When he was finished she took the soap from his hand and with her mouth still locked on his, soaped his back, ending at his loins. Releasing the soap, she took him in one hand, thoroughly soaped his groin, then washed him free of suds and gently pulled him to her, joining them, her knees open and around his thighs.

For the first time since they kissed, she released his mouth.

She looked at him, nose to nose. Her face radiated a smile.

"You will have to do the rest, Nick Carter," she said.

Water spilled over the tub and was carried away in a trough that was built for overflow. Waves broke over the side in a steady cadence. The noise of their actions and the sharp cries that escaped her were lost in the mist of the closed room.

When it was over she turned off the faucet and lay back in his arms. It was a long time before either one spoke.

"How did you find out about Tom?" he finally asked.

She told him about the taxi ride and the room at the Intercontinental.

"I want to know how he died," she said, clinging to both his hands as she nestled in his arms beneath the water.

"Shulgin found the villa and killed him."

"The other body was Shulgin?"

"Colonel Vyacheslav Shulgin has been scratched from the human race."

"He was a brute. Given time, too many would have died at his hands," she said, the emotion tensing her shoulder muscles.

He started to knead them, loosing the cords of muscle with gentle hands and hot water. "They've got thousands like him and have been training them for years. They train all their athletic teams, all their diplomatic corps, all the thousands they will import to the West as deep plants. Each will be as deadly as Shulgin and in place will do incredible damage if hostilities break out."

"So you're blown," she said, changing the subject.

"I'm blown. No more Colonel Vladimir Nikolskiy."

"So how do you pass the coordinates to the two majors replacing Shulgin and Rudzutak? I presume Stupar and Rykov—their immediate subordinates—are now in command."

"They are. And I don't know the answer to the first yet. I'm going to try to play the role of informer. I'm not sure yet."

"We have only four days. Better make up your mind fast." She told him about her meeting in the officers' club and finally tracking down Popolov's agent.

"That's great. What's the plan?" he asked.

"You tell me," she said with disgust. "He wouldn't say. I gave him the date, time, and coordinates."

"You did the best you could. No one could have done it better," he said. "I think I know what Popolov's man does for a living and what his assignment was."

She basked in the warmth of his arms and his compliments while he gave her final instructions. "I have to go to the rebel camp once more."

"What for? It seems to me you're babying them," she said. Her voice was low and sensuous. Her mind wasn't entirely on the rebels.

"They're like children in many ways. And they're too proud for their own good. I have to see them one more time before the battle."

FOURTEEN

"Odah has insisted you have the best tent in the camp. She set it up for you in a wadi, apart from the rest of us." Haami said, beaming at him, showing his smoke-blackened teeth. "She is right to treat you well. We are all grateful to you for your help, Mr. Carter and for her life."

Hafi Amin sat across the fire from them. He nodded and added his thanks. "What do you think will happen now?" he asked.

"Now? I think the long ride has put grit in my eyes and sores where I sit, Hafi, my friend. Now I think I will take advantage of the tent Odah provided."

Both men laughed along with him. Amin repeated his question. "You should sleep. But one minute, friend. Tell us what you think the two enemy camps will do now."

"They will do what I tell them to do."

"What hold over them do you have? What kind of magic is this?" Haami asked.

"No magic, my friend," Carter said, stifling a yawn. "As a Soviet colonel with much power I was able to fool them. But that is past. It won't work again. Now I will play the role Odah cast me in when I arrived. I will pretend to be a traitor to you, but I will give them incorrect information."

"I understand. But what happens now?" Amin asked, the show of persistence characteristic of him.

They were sitting around a small fire in a cleft between towering rocks. The wind whistled around their heads but not where they sat. Smoke curled aloft from the fire. They could not be heard and they could hear nothing but the wind. The dry wood, a precious commodity at this time of year, gave off a pleasant smell.

"The man who planned the scheme to kidnap you also set up a mechanism to make it fail," he said. "A confederate of mine has learned what the plan is. The man who will carry it out has been given false information by my people."

"One last thing, Mr. Carter," Amin said, rising with him. "Our men are restless. With so few Russians camped near us, they are eager to attack."

"I hope my message is clear," Carter said, his tone leaving no doubt as to the gravity of his words. "They must not attack. It is important that we let the enemy carry out my plan. You must permit no mistake in this. One hothead among us will destroy my work."

"But why is it so important to do it your way?" Haami asked. "I have not been sure of this from the first."

Carter knew he would have to make it absolutely clear in terms they understood. "It is face," he explained. "If we organize an attack and kill them, it will be just another skirmish, one of thousands in the last eight years, unimportant. And remember, we will lose many good men." He waited for that to sink in. "But if we do it my way, they will help destroy themselves. Their enormous loss of face will be known around the world. The publicity will bring you much support, perhaps direct intervention from my government." He paused again to make his last point. "And we will lose few men in the process. It will be your greatest victory."

"Will you lead us, Mr. Carter?" the Afghan leader asked.

"At first I thought that would be the best way," Carter explained carefully. "But I have discussed this with my people. We have decided that this action should be your honor and the honor of your men. The enemy will be there for the taking. We will make sure you have the weapons, every kind you need. But no, I will not be with you."

"My men will be pleased at the face you have given us," Haami said. "I will make sure no one moves without my express order."

"My friends, I hope I am not being impolite. Your hospitality has been the best, but now I must sleep," he said through a yawn.

"It is we who are ungracious. We apologize," Haami said, rising. "Sleep well, friend Carter."

Carter found the tent in the wadi. The wadi was like a dry gulch near the camp but at its lowest point. It curled left and right where water cut through the earth on those few occasions when there was a heavy rain. The tent was secluded, protected from prying eyes by the curve of the dry water course.

Carter was impressed by the number of goat hides on the floor and the regal assortment of soft cushions around the walls. He closed the flap against the night winds, peeled off his clothes, and slipped between the extra skins provided to keep him warm. He was asleep almost before his head was down.

With the women in tents nearby, he dreamed of the night with Marianne, the heat of her, the silken feel of her skin. The dream was so real he felt her hand grasp him. He began to swell and fill her hand.

The heat was there, and the gentle nibbling of teeth at his throat. When he felt the cones of her breasts harden against his back, he open his eyes to the reality that there was a Muslin woman in his bed, an unmarried Afghan woman was supposed to be a virgin.

"What the hell . . .?" he blurted out, then kept his voice low. "You shouldn't be here, Odah! What if they find you here?"

"I have women posted. We are all conspirators, we women who cast our eyes to the ground in subjugation. But we are rebels too. We get what we want," she said, the breath of her mouth hot on his neck. "Did you think I would forget just because I let you dissuade me at the cave?"

Carter felt strange turning a woman from his bed, but he had no choice. Odah's being with him there was absolutely unthinkable. But under the circumstances, to turn her down would crush her. He had to do it with grace. At this stage of the operation all he needed was the wrath of a woman scorned.

"We cannot and we must not," he said, taking her by the shoulders and making sure her wrap was secure.

She looked at him with big brown eyes as tears started to fall. "I am ugly," she whispered. "You do not want me."

"It is the law of your people, the respect I have for your father, the respect I have for you," he said, pushing her gently toward the tent flap. He kissed her cheek.

"At any other time, in any other place, I would glory in your offer. You are both beautiful and desirable."

Suddenly she shook from his grasp. Her eyes were wild and her hair in disarray. She reached for the flap and hissed: "You will be sorry, Mr. Nick Carter. You will remember this day."

Carter was awakened by a hand on his shoulder. "Jalaludin Haami commands your presence at his fire," was all the man said.

Dammit! Someone must have seen Odah leave his tent. What was he going to tell her father? In their eyes the fact that she had been in his tent was unforgivable. In some Muslim societies men were beheaded for adultery and women stoned. They might think he had slept with her. If he saw the women gathering stones on the way to Haami's fire, he'd have to find Odah and take off. He took his time with the shirt and pants. The long length of cloth that was his turban wouldn't behave in his hands. It took three tries before he got it right. He slipped into his sandals and walked slowly up the trail from the wadi to the heights of the leaders' fire.

Haami and Amin were not seated. Their dates and bread sat by the fire, uneaten. They were both highly agitated.

"Carter!" Haami bellowed. "This is unbelievable! I cannot remember being in such a rage!"

Carter stood aside and waited. His weapons were in place

but he didn't want to use them on his friends. "Two of our patrols have taken independent action. They have gone after the Russians," Amin explained.

"The fools!" Carter said, relieved one second and enraged the next. "We've got to go after them. If they make contact, it could ruin my plan."

"What do you need?" Haami asked.

"A dozen of your best men. They must know the country, really know it. Give all of them mounts."

He ran for his own horse, grabbed an M-16 that was handed to him by a young rebel, and flung himself into the saddle.

Odah was dressed and out of her tent when she heard the news. She mounted beside him, her rifle slung over one shoulder.

"You're not going," he said simply.

"I am a commander here. You do not order me," she shot back at him.

He rode to Haami's fire where the dozen men were mounted and waiting. "I want only these men, none other," he said, indicating the mounted woman with toss of his head.

"Odah will not be with you," Haami said. He turned to his daughter. "You will dismount and wait for me in your tent," he ordered.

She moved her reins to the right and took off at a gallop, away from the camp, in the opposite direction from the enemy.

"Do not concern yourself with my headstrong daughter. I will send men after her and she will be confined here," he said.

"Good. I will not be responsible for her in battle," Carter said. It was not that he didn't trust her as a soldier, but he did not want to see her taken by the enemy again. He turned his horse to the left and headed down the hill, past his tent and toward Soltankhel.

The Afghan fighters suggested that they follow Wadi Azurkan toward Soltankhel. Carter rode beside a tall thin man about his age. He looked like a fierce fighter, bearded, the black hair showing beneath his turban streaked with gray. He was called Saki Haji Nadir but preferred simply Haji, a name given to those who had been to Mecca on the pilgrimage.

"Do you know any of the men in the patrols that left the camp, Haji?" Carter asked.

"One, Mr. Nick. I trusted him with my life many times. The black American, Ahmed Shah."

Carter was surprised. "I thought he was a level-headed type. Why would he do this?"

"I do not know, Mr. Nick." Haji said sadly.

"And the others?" Carter asked. "Do you know them?"

Haji hesitated before he spoke. They were following the sandy course of the wadi at little more than a walk. Trackers were out front, scouring the ground for prints. "Maybe twenty men. Young hotheads. Stupid men who obey very poorly," he finally replied. "Allah only knows why they have tried it. I have seen them run under fire."

"Not your local heroes, right?"

"Perhaps they think they will catch small patrols and return as heroes," Haji offered.

"The enemy are the finest fighting men the Russians can produce," Carter said. "They are not the homesick boys you have faced before. Every man was the best in his regiment, hand-picked, men who know a thousand ways to kill."

"They have been in battle before?" Haji asked.

"That's a good question. I don't know. I know they trained on helpless prisoners in prison camps. In the process they have killed, but I don't know if they have faced a worthy enemy."

He thought about it for a minute before he added, "It doesn't matter, really. They are fanatics. They will not be stopped unless we kill them. And that will take a lot more than a few men afoot."

Carter's words were lost in the call from the front of the column. "Footprints. Our men. Perhaps two hours old," one of the older men up front shouted.

"Two hours," Carter mused aloud. "We are less than an hour from either camp. They will be very close."

"We would have heard gunfire," Haji said. "They have not engaged."

"Don't be so sure," Carter said. "If they have been spotted, the Russians are capable of taking twenty men without a sound. We could be riding into a trap."

"I'll order the men to ride with their safeties off and be ready to fire quickly," Haji suggested.

"And shoot our own men in the back?" Carter asked. "You know your men well, friend," he added quickly, not wanting a sulking commander on his hands. "I might do the same in battle. But let's see what we are shooting at, then take action. Tell them to look for anything strange. Change the formation to single file at intervals of twenty feet. Keep them in the middle of the wadi. Avoid the trees on the banks."

Haji moved off, leaving Carter alone. The Killmaster had a bad feeling about this action. The hair at the back of his neck told him someone was out there watching. He didn't know whether it was friend or foe.

They rounded a sharp curve in the wadi and found one of rebels. He was pinned to a dead palm trunk, upside down, one arm pointing like a sign.

The men muttered among themselves. Carter was reminded of Tom Petit's death. He could see that the men with him were undecided. But they went on. A hundred feet along the wadi they found a second sign. It was a severed arm with the fingers pointing the way.

"I see no sign of the enemy, Mr. Nick," Haji said. "It is as if they were taken by ghosts."

Carter dismounted. He examined the ground around the tree holding the severed arm. The sand was too smooth. It contained small scrapings, the faint signs of branches used to hide any sign. He persisted. Twenty feet from the severed arm he found a footprint and a trail leading away from the scene. He called Haji to him.

"A boot mark," he explained. "A special boot worn only by the Spetsnaz. See the dotted pattern of the soles? It gives them traction in any terrain, but it also tracks dirt into clean areas. I wore them when I infiltrated their camp."

"Who is this Spet— . . . What is it?" Haji asked.

"*Spetslnaya Nazncheniya,* in Russian. It means special force, or special soldiers . . . the best."

Haji was thoughtful as he bent to examine the print. "It is best if we do not tell my men," he said. "They are brave men, but they are braver when I tell them as little as possible about the enemy."

"The dead men frighten them, do you think?" Carter asked.

"A man is a fool who knows no fear, Mr. Nick."

"Amen."

"What?"

"I said, Allah is wise in the ways of men. Just as Haji Nadir is wise in the ways of men."

The sound of small-arms fire broke out near them. The first three men in their column fell. At the same time, Odah broke from a clump of brush at the edge of the wadi behind them, her M-16 at the ready. She was shouting a war cry as she passed them.

"Odah!" Carter shouted. He could not be heard over the sound of gunfire. He spurred his mount and after a hard ride caught up to her. He was reaching for her reins when she swung the butt of her automatic rifle, catching him in the ribs.

Carter landed on his rump on the hardpan. The shock of the fall jarred him from head to foot and reminded him of the bruised groin he'd brought out of Moscow.

He sprang to his feet and tried to follow her progress. He saw one of the enemy in the distance. The soldier's AK-47 had a light brown plastic butt, of Finnish manufacture, better than the Russian version. He'd seen them in the Spetsnaz camp.

The enemy soldier fired. Odah's horse took a three-round burst and went down. She was out of sight in enemy territory and either hit or unconscious.

Carter looked behind him. Eight of the men with him had turned when they'd seen three of their own shot from the saddle. That left him with Haji and eight others to face the whole Spetsnaz garrison.

"We must go on! We must get to Haami's daughter!" Haji yelled, handing Carter the reins to his horse. The brave Afghan was shaking with fear but was determined to go ahead.

"How far is it back to camp?" Carter asked.

"Seven, perhaps eight miles," Haji said. "Why, Mr. Nick? We will go on, yes?"

"We have eight men and we can't be sure of them. The others are either dead or captured," Carter said sadly. "No. We don't go on, my brave friend. You will take my horse and I will go on foot to scout them."

"But, Mr. Nick . . ."

"No. You will listen. It is important that you listen. I need someone to tell Haami and Amin exactly what happened. All the details," he said, making sure he was understood. "Tell them I have to know what has happened to their people, so I will go on alone."

"But alone, Mr. Nick? What can you—?"

"I have to know who is alive and who is dead," Carter interrupted. "Haami will want to know about Odah," he went on. "I will return and then we will decide how we will get back the ones who are alive. Tell Haami that."

FIFTEEN

The radio was small enough to conceal in a hollowed-out book but was not big enough for long-distance transmission. Marianne could reach the American embassy in Karachi. They would patch her in to the AXE satellite network.

The connection was through faster than she expected. She hadn't asked for Hawk but for Howard Schmidt, AXE's Operations man who had set her up with almost any information or intelligence hardware she'd needed over the years.

"Marianne?" he said. "How's it going? How's Nick?"

"I don't see all that much of him. He runs back and forth to the rebel camp like a shuttle train. He's all right."

"Glad to hear it. What's up?"

"I've got a tactical problem, Howard, and not much time."

"Okay. Shoot."

"Can you get a few hand-held SAM missiles on the next shipment of arms out of Pakistan?"

"The kind that troops use for ground to air?"

"That's what you taught me," she said with a tinge of sarcasm. Schmidt had that one coming. He sometimes treated women agents like idiots when it came to armament.

"How many and when?"

"At least a dozen, and tomorrow if you can make it."

He was silent for a few seconds. "Do you realize we don't even supply these to some of our closest allies? They give the holder too much power. One of those babies can destroy a fifty-million-dollar aircraft!"

"That's the general idea, Howard," she said dryly. "We were told to make this job work. And it was suggested we give the Afghan rebels some face. The SAMs will do that, believe me."

"They have to be taken in by donkey," he said. "I need a week."

"We don't have a week, Howard. Can't you fly some by chopper to a mule train already in the passes? They could off-load some of their cargo, and the chopper could take it back for the next load."

"Will do. Look for it in two days—three at the most."

"Make it two, sweetie. We can handle that."

"I guess. You want Hawk to know?"

She thought about the questions for a few seconds. "Why not?" she finally replied. "It's his show."

"That's it?" he asked.

"For now," she said, closing on a warmer note. "The uniforms are fabulous, Howard. Nick, Tom, and I have been able to go anywhere we want in them. Fabulous."

"All part of the service," he said. "I heard about Tom Petit. I'm real sorry, Marianne. I liked the little guy. He was a talented agent. We'll miss him."

"Me too. A bad business," she said. "Over and out, Howard."

"Take care of yourselves," he said as the transmission faded.

Haji had taken the others back to camp as Carter had ordered. The road the Soviets had taken was no more than a goat track made wider by the military force that Carter followed at a distance. They were on foot. It was impossible to see if they had prisoners from the tracks they left.

Carter raced ahead, through a narrow wadi paralleling their

march. The floppy sandals he wore made the going tougher. After five miles his feet were cut and blistered.

They kept up a fast pace, making him break into a trot to see the whole column at the same time. He crouched behind a pile of rocks halfway up a hill and used Haami's glasses to look them over.

The whole outfit was on the march. They must have been out on an exercise when the rebels hit them.

Suddenly Carter drew in his breath as he looked through the field glasses.

It *wasn't* the Spetsnaz: it was the KGB! Major Stupar, the second in command, was at the head of the column setting the pace. The brute of a man looked as if he could go on forever.

The Killmaster could feel his blood boil. In the middle of the column Odah was tied to other prisoners, a half-dozen bedraggled little men, all tied to each other at the neck and ankles. They were forced to keep up the pace, shuffling along, kicking up dust, their feet cut and bleeding. Carter's powerful glasses picked up the trickle of blood at Odah's neck where the rope cut into her flesh.

He counted the KGB men. Apart from Stupar, another major, and a captain, both following immediately behind him, Carter's tally was a hundred and ninety men and four non-coms. A sergeant major brought up the rear.

The odds were impossible. He might be able to create a diversion and make a try for Odah, but he couldn't help the others. He thought again: the odds would still be too long. It had to be done another way, back in Kabul.

Time was his enemy now. He had to get back to the rebel camp, confer with Haami and Amin, and race back to Kabul on the fastest horse they had.

He turned to run. The narrow wadi joined up with Wadi Azurkan about five miles back. Then it was nine or ten back to camp. If he kept up the pace he would make it in about two hours.

As he ran through the rough sand and gravel of the wadi bed, thoughts flew through his brain. This time Odah would suffer for her foolishness and, he was sure the others would die. He had seen Ahmed Shah among the prisoners. He would probably be treated the worst of all when they found he was an American; the KGB were masters at torture and pain.

His legs churned faster, eating up the miles, sweat pouring from the heavy turban on his head. He pulled it off and wrapped the yards of cloth around his waist as he ran. It was not his job to run around the country saving Odah, but he had to do it. Haami would be frantic. He would not be himself as long as his daughter was in the hands of the KGB. The well-laid plan Carter was about to put into play would be impossible if the rebel leaders didn't cooperate.

It was late afternoon by the time he got back to the rebel camp, but he saw no smoke from cooking fires. He raced to the leaders' campsite: it was empty. They had realized their danger and had moved already. He stood looking for signs, his tortured lungs burning.

They hadn't had time to cover their tracks. He followed the exodus for another five miles, five that felt like fifty. It was almost dark. Rocks he'd have been able to see a half hour ago seemed to jump up at his shredded feet and add to the pain.

He was on the first sentry before he knew it. The man lifted his dusty M-16 and swung it in an arc at the onrushing man.

"Wait!" he shouted, waving his arms. "It's me, Carter! Take me to Haami as fast as you can!"

Marianne sat in the bedroom of the luxurious villa. The place was a safe haven but it bothered her. To use faucets of gold when the Afghan people were fighting for their lives disturbed her.

She had done all that Carter had asked of her. But it wasn't her nature to sit idle and wait for the finale. There had to be something she could do while Carter was away.

Transport. She couldn't use the Rolls-Royce that the Afghan diplomat had left behind. The Jeep Wagoneer would be too conspicuous. They'd be better off with something military. She still had her uniform. She'd find a dim-witted noncom and expropriate a vehicle.

What about Carter's last bit of business that was still not done, infiltrating the two enemy camps and planting the time and coordinates for the attack? She decided not to act on that. He knew the ground better than she, and he might have plans she could screw up. She figured she'd better leave that one alone.

There was one other thing she could do, however: talk to young Ibrahim. She could get a line of clothes and uniforms for Carter for when he returned. She didn't know if it would help, but it was better than sitting on her hands.

Jalaludin Haami sat the the fire, his legs crossed, his head in his hands. Hafi Amin sat next to him, his hand on his friend's shoulder.

"This senseless grief will not bring her back, old friend," he said. "It is the will of Allah."

Carter sat impatiently. He had not run his guts out to sit through a scene like this when he should be on his way back to Kabul. He had to find a suitable new front, something so believable that Stupar would be convinced to give up his prisoners. He'd been racking his brain but hadn't come up with the answer yet. Getting back to the city, setting up the scam, and pulling it off would take time, and he didn't have enough time. The clock was already ticking. Popolov's man had been briefed. It was too late to change. They had less than three days.

"Haami, old friend," he said, breaking in on the exclamations of grief. "I got her back once. I can do it again."

"They will be waiting for you," the old man said. He raised his head and ran his hands through his beard, uncertain what to do with them. "It is a matter of face for us now. We must go after our own."

This was just what Carter feared. It was the reason he'd run all the way back. He'd been afraid that Haami would be on the trail of his daughter by the time he'd returned to the camp.

"You forget what we discussed. They must not capture you.

Not ever! If they do, all the resistance in your land will probably cease," Carter said. "Think of it. The Russians will have won. Let me handle it."

He looked at the old man, captured his eyes, and held them with his. "I make a promise to you," he said, his voice firm. "We will lead a force that will see the death of them all by your hand. I guarantee it."

"And how will this come to pass, *kawajah*?"

They sat for a moment without speaking. The insult had come naturally to the old man's lips. Carter, despite his heroics, was an outsider, an infidel, and the Afghans never forgot it. Only a man like Ahmed Shah, a man who had become a Muslim, prayed with them five times a day, fasted during Ramadan, paid the zakat to the poor, and accepted Allah as the one true God, could be accepted as one of them.

"What is it you want to do?" Amin asked, breaking the silence.

"I need a fast horse back to Kabul. I must assume the role of a traitor and seek her out."

"And in the time it takes, my Odah will be dead, or worse," the old man said, tears streaming down the face that was normally strong and resolute.

"You may be right," Carter conceded, "but it is our only choice. I need a horse and a guide, someone to take me through the dark to Kabul as fast as possible."

"I am not sure that is the way," Amin said.

"Then wallow in your self-pity, old man," Carter said, trying to shake him out of his stubborn grief. "I'll take a horse and a guide, the man Haji Nadir. If you are as foolish as the men who cause this problem, you will not be here when I return with your daughter. And all of Afghanistan will fall."

He stood up and stomped from the fire. He found Haji talking with friends around a campfire drinking tea and telling the usual lies about the battles he'd fought and the woman he'd had. Carter talked to him briefly, cut out two horses, and was mounted in less than ten minutes. As they headed out, the figure of Jalaludin Haami blocked their way.

"May Allah be with you," he said, holding out a hand to Carter.

"And may Allah bless you and yours this day," the man from AXE replied as he led the way to Kabul and a job that all but impossible.

SIXTEEN

Carter and Haji left their horses with a peasant farmer outside Kabul and took a taxi to within three blocks of the new safe house. The trip had taken a third of the time it had taken Carter to find the camp on his first trip. Haji had known shortcuts, and the animals had been pushed unmercifully. Carter had hated to mistreat them, but they would survive. Odah and the rebels might not.

Carter had arranged a signal system with Marianne. She appeared at the front gates in the uniform of a Soviet officer of the Kremlin Guard. Haji swung his M-16 on her in alarm, but he settled down when she addressed him in Pashto. The shock of the meeting was less than his reaction when she removed a false nose and took off the uniform to reveal an attractive young woman underneath. It was almost too much for him. He sat and drank tea as they talked, feasting his eyes on her face, a pleasure that was denied him in his society.

"What in heaven's name is wrong with that girl?" Marianne blurted out when Carter told her of the latest development. "She's going to screw this up for sure."

Carter might have told her the truth, but he felt it better that Haji not know. "She's headstrong, and I guess something must have set her off."

151

"Something or someone," she said, giving him a nudge that Haji couldn't see. "What the hell are we going to do now?"

In deference to Haji they had been speaking in Pashto.

"I'm going to try to get them out," Carter said.

"They're probably dead already. Or close to it."

"I've got to try. If the rebels attack in anger before our plan takes shape, they could blow the whole thing."

"Do you have a cover?" she asked.

"I thought I'd go in as a native Afghan."

"I've got some uniforms and some business suits for you. Your friend Ibrahim supplied them. And I have my makeup case. You can be anyone you want." She thought about it for a few seconds. "You've heard of the Serbsky Institute," she said. It wasn't a question.

He nodded. He'd run into some of their graduates. The school was the most infamous training facility in the Soviet Union, and its course of study dealt with methods of interrogation.

"You want me to pose as one of them?" he asked.

"Why not?" she replied. "The rebels are going to be interrogated. Isn't it natural for General Lorkh to send in a specialist who happens to be visiting from Moscow?"

"Good idea. I can't think of anything better."

"Okay. We'll try to make you as innocuous as possible: a nondescript suit, an oversize greatcoat, a battered felt hat. Maybe we could fatten up your cheeks," she said. "And give you a Stalin mustache."

Haji looked on, fascinated, as the transformation proceeded.

"Stupar is isolated from Lorkh," she said as whe worked. "How did you find out about the prisoners?" she asked, thinking about firming up his new cover.

"Lorkh has a surprisingly good intelligence network. We were lucky to fool him as long as we did," Carter said, starting to feel uncomfortable with the new plastic cheeks she was applying. "He's got a pipeline into both camps."

"Igor Leonid Grusha," she said. "That's your new name."

"Grusha. As good as any," he said, examining his new appearance in a mirror. "Haji will drive for me. Give him a uniform. A corporal maybe. Or a sergeant."

"I thought I'd drive for you."

"No way. I want you to get a four-wheel-drive vehicle and catch up with the donkey train from Pakistan," he said, holding up a hand to cut off her objection. "It's vital we get Howard's shipment in time. He's also sending me a video camera and a battery pack. Familiarize yourself with it. When you've got it all together meet me at the rebel camp."

"Chauvinist pig," she said, half meaning it.

"C'mon, Marianne, this isn't busywork. If I don't show up in time, you know the time and coordinates. You lead them in and then keep clear. Make sure you get it all on tape."

The thought sobered her. He was right. Being the backup was important. She'd played the role often enough to know that. "You're right," she said, resigned. "You're always right."

He looked at her fondly and took one of her hands despite the presence of the Afghan. "I wish that were true, Marianne, I wish that were true."

Two of the men were hanging from a beam by the neck. They had been dead for several hours. Carter's stomach lurched when he thought of Odah's fate. He steeled himself for the sight of her.

They were walking from one small room at another. Major Stupar had evacuated some of his men from the crude cubicles and turned them into interrogation rooms

"We were unsuccessful with those two, Comrade Grusha," Stupar said. "I have not been to your facility for a few years. The skill diminishes with time."

"It is important work for the party, Comrade Major. We should all keep our skills intact," Carter said, almost choking on the words. He hated this kind of role. To play any role successfully you had to get the feel of it, to really get into the character. This one made him sick to his stomach. As a specialist from the Serbsky Institute, he had to have tortured to death hundreds of dissidents or prisoners personally.

They continued to the next room. Ahmed Shah lay on a rough wooden table. He was still breathing, but unable to talk.

"This one was difficult," Stupar said. "The drugs were too powerful."

Carter knew what he meant. Shah's brain would be fried. He'd be a vegetable. "You overdosed this one, comrade. I can see it in his eyes. No matter. I have a drug that will restore his memory for a few hours. After that . . . it doesn't matter, does it?" He laughed, a wheezy cackle he had practiced with Marianne's help before leaving the villa. "Of course, I'll have to take them all back to General Lorkh's headquarters for best results."

"I'd prefer to keep them here," Stupar objected.

"General Lorkh's orders," Carter said. "They will produce more in a better environment. Really, Major," Carter said, waving a gloved hand around the room. "You do work in the most primitive conditions."

"You cannot always choose," Stupar muttered.

"You are in full charge of this group now?" Carter asked as they walked on to the next room.

"Yes. Our original commander—Colonel Shulgin—was killed by rebel bandits. It happens to our brave men all too often in this hellhole."

"Hellhole, comrade? You'd better not let them hear you say that in Moscow."

"I didn't mean anything against our leaders, Comrade Grusha. I only meant—"

"I know. It *is* a hellhole. I'm sure our leaders would pull out if they could save face," Carter said. "I will tell my superiors that you cooperated fully. Do not worry."

Stupar opened another door and Carter finally saw her. She was tied by her wrists to the posts of a crude bed. She appeared to be unharmed and was still breathing. Carter's gut ached with tension.

"I have only a driver and a staff car, Major. I'll need a truck and a driver. I'll send them back from Kabul."

"Will you let me know what success you have as soon as possible? It might have a great bearing on my mission," Stupar said. He spoke tentatively, unsure of his ground. Men like Grusha were anathema to him. Even with his status as a major in the KGB, the Grushas of his world troubled him.

In fifteen minutes a Zil-131 troop carrier was standing in front of Stupar's headquarters. The prisoners were in back. Haji had driven the staff car to the front of the truck and sat ramrod stiff at the wheel, obviously hoping no one would speak to him in Russian.

Carter made a show of inspecting the truck. The worst of the prisoners were bundled in blankets on the floor. Three men sat, dazed, holding on to struts within the truck, staring straight ahead. A Russian corporal sat behind the wheel awaiting his signal to move out.

Stupar appeared and saluted as Carter climbed into his car, then they pulled out. Dust streamed out behind the small convoy as they moved out of sight of the camp. After four miles of almost impossible roads, Carter called for a halt. He told the Russian driver to have a smoke while he checked the prisoners. The corporal jumped from the truck and pissed against the stump of a dead tree while Carter walked to the back.

"Can any of you drive?" he whispered in Pashto.

One of the men who were sitting up looked at him in surprise and nodded.

"I am a friend of Jalaludin Haami, posing as a Russian," Carter whispered. "If you can drive, I will kill the driver and you will follow me to safety."

The man nodded again and prepared to jump down.

"Wait," Carter commanded softly. He walked behind the Russian driver, still facing the tree stump, and smashed him on

the head with the butt of his Luger. He dragged the unconscious man behind a clump of brush at the side of the road and
returned to the truck.

"You will drive now," he told the Afghan. "Wait for my
signal."

When the driver was gone, he turned to the other two
Afghan rebels. "Are you fit enough to handle a rifle?" he
asked.

At the prospect of holding arms, they brightened, seemed to
come out of their trancelike state, and told him they could.

Carter walked to the trunk of the staff car and opened it. He
thought of Petit, "the scrounger," as he lifted out the weapons
that the small man's contact Ibrahim had supplied.

He carried a Soviet Rocket-Propelled Grenade Type 7, a
RPG-7, to the back of the truck. "Can you handle this? What
is your name?" he asked.

The man grinned at the sight of the weapon. He assumed a
prone position, elbows and knees against the bed of the truck,
his feet turned sideways, acting as props, and help the RPG-
7 as if it were an old friend. "I am called Ahmed," he said as
he shoved the 80mm rocket grenade in the 40mm tube. He
looked through the telescopic sight and grinned again. "Are
you expecting trouble?" he asked.

"I am a cautious man," Carter said. He passed a loaded AK-
47 to the other man. The soldier smiled and held the weapon
expertly, sliding the cocking lever back and forth, ejecting a
couple of shells as he held the gun at the ready. "Major Stupar
had a strange look on his face as we pulled away," he told
them. "I'm not taking chances."

He returned to the car, tossed a Kalashnikov beside Haji,
another AK-47 and an RPG-7 in the back seat for himself, then
closed the trunk and gave the signal to pull out.

The old Zil transport was unable to make more than fifteen
miles an hour. They were halfway to the rebel camp when it
happened. From out of their dust at the rear a staff car
appeared, ordering them to stop.

The Afghan had been in too many firefights to respond to such an order. Before Carter even knew the staff car was behind, Ahmed had loosed an 80mm grenade point-blank and had blown the staff car off the road.

"Get off the road behind those trees!" Carter ordered.

The Russian car described an arc in the air and slid to a stop on its roof. The stink of burning rubber filled the air. He saw four men pile from the staff car. They were dazed but still heavily armed. The hulking form of Stupar was one of them. Two bodies still sat in the front seat. Their faces had been turned to pulp.

A withering hail of fire was directed at the back of the old truck. The Afghans responded with fire of their own. Another 80mm grenade demolished the staff car, but the four surviving occupants were long gone.

Carter fired at the muzzle flashes where the Russians had taken cover. He saw one man get hit and fall back. The gunfire from the truck had ceased; a Russian grenade had made a direct hit in the interior of the truck.

Two Russians tried to circle around and get at Carter from the side. He tossed down the empty AK-47, held his Luger in his right hand, and shot the two men in the head as they tried to sneak behind a group of boulders.

After the constant chatter of small-arms fire and the explosions from the grenades, the barren landscape was ominously quiet. Carter looked at his staff car and saw Haji sitting rigidly at the wheel. The automatic rifle was held loosely in hands already turning cold. A string of 7.56mm slugs had been stitched all along the car, taking out the glass and the driver.

Carter sensed he was not alone. Of the four Russians, he had seen only three go down. He knew that all his people in the truck were gone. There was no chance anyone could have survived.

Suddenly Carter saw something move behind a boulder where the first Russian had been hit.

"Stupar! Are you still with us?" he called in Russian.

"I am not easy to kill, Carter."

"You know who I am."

"The Afghans jabbered so much I almost missed it. Carter. The great Killmaster. Anyone in the KGB of importance knows of you," he yelled. "And I will have the pleasure of killing you."

The problem now was whether Stupar had told anyone else. Carter had to find out. "So all of Moscow knows you will be bringing me in," he called back.

"They will know when I have you. Only a fool announces victories beforehand no matter how certain," he shouted. "But I will get you, American. You have nowhere to go."

A long silence followed. Carter had nothing to add. He had to find out more.

"I suspect you were the one who killed Colonel Shulgin," Stupar finally went on. "General Lorkh has been a fool. He has put blinders on us all, but no more."

Carter had gradually squirmed to the car and eased out the RPG-7. It was loaded and cocked. It had a range of five hundred yards at stationary targets and a minimum safe range of fifty yards for the operator. Stupar was only thirty yards away. Maybe the recoil would be too great.

To hell with it, Carter thought. He couldn't take a chance on Stupar getting loose and blowing his cover. The Russian should have done it when he had the chance.

He aimed slightly to the left of the rock where Stupar was hiding, at another rock a few yards behind. The range finder showed his target at just over thirty-five yards and a red caution light glowed. The launcher knew better than he that he could be a victim if he let go from this range.

The rocket whooshed off on a straight line, leaving a trail of heat and smoke behind. The explosion knocked him back against the car. Blackness descended on him as the noise hurting his ears disappeared and he fell through a long tunnel that was as black as a moonless night and silent as the grave.

Carter opened his eyes to see a monster standing over him

blocking out the light. Most of the man's uniform had been blown from his body. His back must have been filled with shrapnel, but there he stood.

In one hand he held a commando knife, the only weapon not blasted into the brush and sand around him.

Carter looked around desperately. Wilhelmina was under the car, half covered with sand. He stood groggily, expecting the commando knife to sink into his flesh momentarily, but he felt nothing.

He managed to get to his feet and stood, shaking his head when the first attack came. He ducked and heard the knife clang off the metal of the car behind him.

Hugo appeared in his hand as if by magic. It was a trick he'd practiced a thousand times until the stiletto came to him automatically in an emergency.

The two men circled, neither one fully recovered from the concussion of the grenade. The sun beat down on them, a winter sun that did not have the debilitating power it had in summer, but it was hot enough to affect two wounded men.

They circled warily, their feet scuffing the dust, creating small clouds, the smell of blood strong on the wind, attracting turkey buzzards that circled overhead.

Stupar lunged, slitting Carter's greatcoat the length of his arm. The stiletto in the Killmaster's other hand came up quickly, penetrating under the major's armpit, cutting through tendons, making the arm useless.

Stupar switched the blade to the other hand and charged. He crushed Carter against he car, knocking the wind from him. Again, darkness descended and he slid down the car, landing on his rump, barely conscious.

Hugo was no longer in his right hand. His confused brain thought about it. His hands pushed aside the dirt looking for it. He was too far away to reach for his gun.

The major was not in front of him. As the fog cleared from Carter's brain he struggled to his knees. Stupar was down on his face in front of him, the stiletto sticking out of his back in the midst of a score of shrapnel holes. The kill had been a reflex action. From the look of his back, it was a miracle that the man had been able to stand at all, let alone fight.

Carter pulled himself to his feet. He felt like hell but was not wounded. The explosion had been too close and had scrambled his brain for a few minutes.

Haji was dead. He pulled him out and started the car. Despite the damage, it started immediately. He examined the tires and the gas tank. They had not been hit. His weapons were retrieved, examined, and put away.

Then he smelled smoke. The Zil transport was on fire. With this remaining strength, he ran to the truck and began pulling out bodies.

When he had the piles of blood-soaked blankets and riddled bodies far enough from the truck, he began to examine them.

When the gas tank finally blew, it sent fire out in a radius of fifty feet, but Carter was far enough away to go on with his job. Ahmed Shah was dead. His brain and been irreversibly damaged by drugs, but he'd also caught a slug through the head.

The man who'd handled the grenade rocket had taken two bullets through the chest. The others were riddled with small-arms fire and shrapnel, their bodies torn by the grenade.

The last of the blankets held Odah. It smoldered, all charred at one end. He was afraid of what he would find.

He unrolled the blanket gently. Her chest still rose and fell rhythmically, but with little strength. Both her feet were badly burned. The blanket was soaked with blood, but he couldn't see any major wounds.

Carter figured he was halfway between Kabul and the rebel camp. He could take Odah to the safe house, but he had no help there. And they would probably be caught on the way: certainly stopped and questioned about a staff car riddled with bullet holes.

Should he continue to the rebel encampment? he wondered. Time was running short. He had to get to the two enemy commanders and make sure they were not in communication with the outside world. And he had to set them up for the final kill.

He didn't have time to take Odah back to her father, but he knew he had to. It meant a full day to get to the camp and then back to Kabul, and he had only two days and a few hours. And he had no idea what he'd find at the camp.

SEVENTEEN

The staff car took them as far as Gardez on the road to Khost. Carter had changed into the best of the available rebel clothes and driven like a madman through the ruts that passed for roads with Odah moaning in the back, her body covered with blankets. He had no drugs for the pain, no dressings for her feet.

He passed two rebel campsites he recognized from previous visits and realized Haami was on the move, leading his people closer to Khost each time some of followers disobeyed his orders and were captured. This was one of the compelling reasons why Carter decided not to lead them into battle. He had no doubt that his plan would work, but total control of the *mujaheddin* was impossible. The nature of the Afghan was to be independent, or to serve a local tribal chief. While they all loved and respected Haami and Amin, their own perceptions of when to fight and when to obey were never predictable. The rebel leaders were right to take evasive action by moving the camp, but time was running out. Carter had less than two days before Popolov's secret weapon would appear at the designated battle area.

Suddenly the car hit a rock, and the camouflaged old car lost its oil pan. Carter pulled Odah from the back seat, slung her over his shoulder, and started walking. He knew they weren't far from the new rebel camp.

It was a particularly hot day for winter. The sun was at its height. As he trudged on, his tattered old clothes stank of the man who had owned them.

"Halt!"

The familiar command was music to his ears. A sentry, a young fighter, too young to sport a beard, was concealed behind a huge boulder, M-16 barrel pointing at Carter's chest.

"I have brought Haami's daughter back from the enemy," Carter announced. "Show yourself, boy."

"Show me her face," the voice answered from behind the rock.

Carter unfolded the blanket. The young lad sucked in his breath. Odah was in shock. Blood matted her hair and had dried on her chin and throat.

"Take me to the tents of the women," Carter commanded.

When they arrived, Carter gave orders for Odah to be cared for and turned to the young man. "Haami will be told only that his daughter had been saved and is resting," he told him. "If I hear that you have told anyone of her condition, *anyone*, I will have you flogged in front of the whole camp."

Wearily he trudged to the fire of the leaders to find them both sitting with Salman Amin, talking strategy as usual.

"Carter!" Haami said, jumping to his feet. "What is the word about my people?" He hesitated for a moment or two. "And my daughter?"

"Odah is with the women. She needs rest," Carter said. "I'm sorry," he said slowly, sitting down and accepting a mug of tea, "the others are all dead."

He told them of the rescue and the firefight. He emphasized that their men had died courageously.

They sat for a moment, thinking of their friends, the fires they had shared and would not share again.

"And my daughter?" Haami asked. "Is she harmed? Did they mistreat her?"

Carter kept his face as expressionless as possible. He had

played the tables of Monte Carlo with the best, and the master bluff was no stranger to him. "She's in good hands," he said. "She suffered burns to her feet in the firefight, but she will survive."

The old warrior looked into his eyes, trying to read another message but saw none. "We will assemble the men and attack the next patrol that heads this way," he said, waving to the teaboy to fill his cup.

"You will stay here until the plan is ready," Carter said coldly.

"And when will this plan we have heard so much about be ready?" Salman Amin asked caustically. "We sit here like children and mourn our dead without taking action. Are we warriors or small boys?" he added, his voice carrying to men sitting at the closest fire. A grumble of assent floated back to them on the evening breeze.

"Men should not sit and talk with the minds of boys," Carter said, holding Salman's eyes with his own. "We will get them all and soon. I need one more trip to Kabul to set it up." He almost added that his last visit to the capital would have been made had it not been for Odah's foolish action.

"Carter is right," Haami said. "We will not risk good men on useless forays. If Carter brings them out in the open at a place of his choosing, we will destroy them."

"You are a man of wisdom," Carter said. "It is time for me to go over the plan with you," he added. He explained that the fight would be much larger than he had originally planned, that they would be using some new and formidable weapons and that he would be back to train some of them. "Pick out a dozen men who have used portable rocket launchers—like the RPL-7. I have some new weapons arriving for them."

"And when exactly is this battle?" Salman asked.

"The day after tomorrow, late in the afternoon. You will need three leaders. One for a small force of a hundred men that will be the decoy, the one in the Center and in the most danger. We will also deploy two larger forces that will decide the battle."

"I will lead the small force," Salman announced.

"I'm not sure," his father said cautiously.

"Salman can handle it," Carter said. "He would be a good choice."

The young man looked at Carter with respect for the first time and smiled.

"If this plan works, the Russians will look bad in newspapers all over the world." Carter stopped to let the words sink in. "If the Russians are embarrassed by our action here, my president has promised much more aide and direct intervention.

"Odah and her men almost spoiled that," he concluded.

"I am truly sorry for my daughter's action, Mr. Carter. What more can I say?"

"What are your plans between now and the time for the battle?" Amin the father asked, changing the painful subject.

"I will be very busy. I must leave you soon," he said. "I have to make sure both enemy forces have received orders for the time and place of the battle. Then I will return to help set up your battle formations."

"And you will not be a part of it?" Salman asked.

"No. My commander advises that my job was to ensure that you remain as leaders of the rebels. When the battle is won, my job is over. He has forbidden me to take the glory of the battle from the men who deserve it."

"You don't have anything to prove to us, Mr. Carter. You are a brave man," Salman said. "I'm sorry I ever doubted you."

"Spoken like a man destined to lead as your father has," Carter said. "But I'll leave you now for a while. I'll be riding out soon."

He started to rise and thought of something else. "I have a confederate who may arrive with the next arms shipment," he told them. "She may appear as a man or a woman. Trust her. She is a proven soldier. I have worked with her many times."

Slowly he rose and left them so they could think about the

coming battle. He knew discussion of this new development would keep their fire burning well into the night.

Carter went to the tent where they had placed Odah. The women parted to let him in, something they wouldn't have done for any other man except her father. But this was the man who had brought her back to them.

"How do you feel?" he asked, kneeling beside her.

She was pale as death. She put a hand on his. It was cold. A chill went down his spine.

He turned to one of the women. "Has she injuries I didn't know about?" he asked.

Tears rolled down the woman's cheeks. She had taken off her veil. She was a middle-aged woman who had probably never shown her face to a stranger. "She has a wound here." She pointed to her own abdomen. "We have no drugs, nothing to ease the pain."

Carter asked them to show him the wound.

She uncovered only the area of the wound. It was an ugly tear five or six inches long, and deep. The piece of shrapnel was still there, and blood oozed from the inflamed tear. She must have picked it up while in the truck and he hadn't seen it. He cursed himself.

"Leave us," Odah commanded, the first words she'd spoken since he entered.

She squeezed his hand. She was very weak. "I want you to forgive me. I have been a fool in many ways."

"A little too eager to be a fighter, perhaps, but not a fool."

"I wanted you to love me," she whispered.

"Tell me, Odah, was I wrong to follow the laws of your people?" he asked, his mouth close to her ear.

"No. You were right. But now it will never happen. I wanted you so and it will never happen."

She squeezed his hand lightly.

He sat with her for a few minutes. She breathed more strongly for a minute or two then slipped into a deep sleep, her breathing slow and shallow. As he was about to leave, she started to rise. Her eyes opened wide, looking beyond him. Her face was radiant, as if she saw something wonderful. She fell back, the smile still on her face.

The women began to wail. The bone-chilling sound filled the tent and was picked up throughout the women's quarters.

He left and went back to the fire. "Promise me you will not leave this camp until I return," he said to the men, looking at each face in turn.

Haami nodded, tears streaming down his face.

The new rebel camp was deeper in the hills, and the ride back to Kabul took longer than the last trip he'd made with Haji. Carter thought hard about events to come.

Before he left, the rebels showed him the hundreds of Russian uniforms they had obtained. They would attack as Russians and get a lot closer because of them.

"The uniforms are a stroke of genius," he told them. "We will use them for Salman's force . . . exactly the touch I've been looking for."

Carter was exhausted. He filled the tub in the villa and stepped into the hot water. Lying there, his thoughts continued. Right now time was his enemy. Tomorrow was the fateful day and he hadn't given either Russian force the time or coordinates for the battle. Captain Vadim Munshin would have succeeded Stupar as the leader of the KGB by now, and Major Alexi Rykov would have firm control of the Spetsnaz.

He didn't have time to infiltrate both camps. He didn't even have time to play the role of informer and get to both camps. He would have to come up with something unique, something that was fast and convincing.

He reached for the phone at the side of the tub and dialed General Lorkh's number.

"General Lorkh's office," a voice answered.

"This is Major Rykov," Carter said. "I must speak to the general immediately."

"I'm sorry, but he's not here, Major. He's inspecting troops in the field."

"You're sure he's not sleeping off too much vodka?" Carter asked.

"Major, I will not pass on such an insult to the general this time, but I advise you to be careful of your tongue in the future."

"Who the hell is this?"

"Lieutenant Persof, sir."

"Well, Persof," Carter said. "As the senior officer, I will give the advice here. You're sure he's in the field? You're not covering for him?"

"Yes, sir."

"Who is the senior officer at headquarters? I will speak to him."

The lieutenant hesitated for a second or two. Carter was beginning to gain some hope for the plan he had in mind.

"Captain Volvanov is at the airfield for the next two hours. I will have him call you."

"You mean you're the ranking officer?" Carter asked.

"I am the senior officer for a short while, sir. The general took most of his staff with him."

"That's a hell of a way to run an army. Never mind. I'll manage without his help," Carter said, slamming down the phone.

Marianne's horse stumbled across another ridge to another pass. It had to be the twentieth or more she'd explored in the last two days. She should have asked Howard Schmidt for some coordinates. Finding the munitions caravan herself was beginning to seem hopeless.

She was just inside the Afghan border and had been searching all the passes from Pakistan. She wondered now what had made her think she could find a munitions caravan by herself when the Russians had tried without success. She sat back on her horse, reached for her glasses, and scanned the craggy peaks for the hundredth time.

She saw movement. The twitching ears of a score of donkeys drew her attention as they picked their way, sure-footed, along a narrow ledge a few miles away. They were heading in the right direction. If they had been met by the helicopter and supplied with the SAMs, her day would be complete.

Carter, after a lightning ten minutes of preparation, was dressed in the uniform of a communications officer recently arrived from the motherland. He had taken a taxi from the villa and had been in Lorkh's headquarters making junior officers jump to his tune for the past half hour. He finished writing on a pad at a desk he'd commandeered and walked to the computer room. He carried two sets of official attack orders and went over them with the operator. "I want you to send them as shown, one to Major Rykov and the other to Captain Munshin," he said to the corporal in charge after reviewing the orders with him. "If you get them mixed up, a lot of our men could be killed and you'll end up in the gulags."

"It will be done, Major."

Carter left them to it. He stayed clear of the officer's mess. He'd been playing two roles around headquarters, and too much exposure would kill him—literally. He expropriated a car and drove to a native restaurant, kept his back to the wall like the gunfighters of old, and ate a meal of chicken and rice.

An hour later he walked into the communications room and picked up his copy of the orders. He made sure no record of his visit remained. He read them over. If he'd had more time, he'd have made each more individual. He would have worded each with less similarity, but it was too late for that. He could only hope the messages had been routed correctly and the recipients would take orders literally.

14.10 HOURS 23 NOVEMBER. MAJOR RYKOV, SPECIAL SPETSNAZ FORCE XXX CONFIRMED THIS OFFICE AS COMMANDER REPLACING RUDZUTAK XXX PLANS OF REBEL LEADERS NOW KNOWN XXX PROCEED WITH ALL RANKS TO COORDINATES 341.622 1800 HOURS 25

NOVEMBER XXX POSITION YOUR FORCE EAST SIDE OF DEFILE XXX ENEMY FORCE WILL BE DUG IN AT THE DEFILE USING UNIFORMS STOLEN FROM OUR DEAD XXX CHANGE OF ORDERS XXX DO NOT KIDNAP LEADERS XXX ATTACK AND DESTROY ALL ENEMY FOUND.

SEGORSKI

The message to Rykov was right, *if* it had been sent out as ordered. He read the other:

14.15 HOURS 23 NOVEMBER CAPTAIN MUNSHIN, SPECIAL KGB FORCE XXX CONFORMED THIS OFFICE AS COMMANDER REPLACING STUPAR XXX PROCEED ALL RANKS TO COORDINATES 341.622 AT EXACTLY 1750 HOURS 25 NOVEMBER. POSITION YOUR FORCE WEST SIDE OF DEFILE XXX ENEMY WILL BE DUG IN AT DEFILE WEARING UNIFORMS STOLEN FROM OUR DEAD XXX CHANGE OF ORDERS XXX DO NOT KIDNAP LEADERS XXX ATTACK AND DESTROY ALL ENEMY FOUND.

GREGAROV

Good. It looked as if it should work. It was a perfect mixture of flattery and command. He doubted if either commander would challenge the order of his supreme commander. Not when he'd just been commended by the top man in his field. He began to feel better about the whole assignment. Now, if he could keep the *mujaheddin* in line, if everything came off as planned, if he could get out with his skin, the job Hawk had given him would be history.

He went back to the villa for the last time and prepared to leave for the last act. While he changed to native robe and turban, he began to have doubts. The whole plan hinged on the KGB and Spetsnaz officers buying the phony orders. The longer he thought about it, the lower he figured the odds.

Carter picked up the phone and called Ibrahim.

"Carter. I'm finished with the villa. You can pick up the extra uniforms and close up."

"Good enough, man," Ibrahim said in English. "How's it going?"

"It could be better," Carter replied. "Any chance you have

a set of dark camouflage fatigues and a bike?"

"Some night work, right?"

"Something like that."

"I've got some black fatigues, but no camouflage. Want some black face makeup?"

Carter laughed to himself at the audacity of the American working under the noses of the Soviets. If Ibrahim could do it, why not the CIA? "Sounds good," he said. "What about a bike?"

"An old Harley-Davidson is all. Driven on Fridays to the mosque by a little old lady."

"I'll be there in fifteen minutes. Have everything ready."

Carter took the bike out into the countryside and stopped to sit on a big rock and let his night vision develop. He was going to both enemy camps in the middle of the night and could not show a light.

It took fifteen minutes but it was worth it. He was able to ride at about thirty miles an hour to the Spetsnaz camp and see every rock and pothole as he sped cross-country to the hilltop stronghold.

This was not a penetration; it wasn't necessary and he hadn't time for it. As it was he barely had time to inspect both camps and get to the rebel camp by dawn.

As he rode, half his attention was on the road and the other half was on what he would find. If the commanders didn't buy his bogus scheme, the Popolov attackers would be the only ones to show up. He'd still have to come up with a plan to destroy the two groups. Either that or discourage them and have them recalled. He would not win either way, but he liked his original plan best.

He could see the Spetsnaz camp from five miles away. It was lit like a baseball diamond during a night game. He kept his eyes on the road to preserve his night vision until he was within a mile of the place.

He wasn't afraid of detection. The big Harley motor was

very quiet. The camp's own noise would hide any noise he made. As he'd hoped, the soldiers appeared to be preparing for battle. With their march only hours away, they weren't planning on enemy infiltration.

Carter stopped on a small rise a mile away. He pulled a rifle from a leather sheath on the bike and sighted on the camp. Ibrahim had equipped the rifle with an AP-4 night vision sight. He panned from left to right. The camp was alive with preparations. He could see Major Rykov at his command headquarters watching the goings-on. He was dressed in camouflage battle dress with all the Spetsnaz weaponry in place. Carter could see every detail on the ten-power scope.

He didn't wait for them to pull out. The ruse had worked, longshot or not. Still, he had to check out the KGB camp. They were the more suspicious force, and it would be natural for them to check out the orders they had received. Still, they were commanded by a captain now. He was probably basking in the good fortune of a new command after the death of both his colonel and major. The personal confirmation by Gregarov would also be on his mind. To check on such an order might take lot of guts for a man with a new command and a battle to face within hours.

Carter turned the Harley, coasted down the hill, and headed for Captain Munshin's command.

Carter pulled into the rebel camp early the next morning. He hadn't slept for more than twenty-four hours, but this was not the time. He had learned what he had to know, and that was worth a couple of nights' sleep. The plan was working.

At the camp the Afghans stood around admiring themselves in the Russian uniforms. They had taken great pains to look like the real thing. Carter's first reaction was to let it go. But both Russian forces were expecting Afghans in Russian army uniforms, and that's what he wanted them to see.

"You'll have to get your officers to sort them out," he told Haami and Amin. "Line them all up and make them swap until none have uniforms that fit."

"But that makes no sense," Haami insisted. "We want them to look as natural as possible. I have ordered them to shave off their beards."

"And that brought out the complaints," Amin added.

"They can forget the shave. We want the enemy to spot them as Afghans posing as Russians right away. It's part of the strategy," Carter explained. "If they see our men at a distance with field glasses and we pass for real Russian troops, we may never get close enough to them to make my plan work."

"You have never told us all of your plan," Haami complained. "We will do the fighting, but you hold back all the details."

"Okay. We have only hours to prepare. I'll make it as clear as I can," Carter said, drawing a map in the sand. "Salman's force will form up in the defile that runs through the battlefield and wait. The two enemy forces will think they have him trapped. He will toss a few grenades at each side as they approach. His people will stay behind the rocks and they'll all pull out as soon as they draw fire from both sides."

"But the Russians might not fall for the decoy," Salman said.

"It doesn't matter. They will be drawn in close enough. Our real force will be much larger. Your father and Haami will select two commanders who will take thousands of men and hide them on either side of the defile, out of sight, at least three miles back. The enemy will not see them until they are trapped in the middle."

"The two commanders will be Hafi and myself," Haami said.

"What's the use of this whole plan to keep you safe if you're going to lead the troops?" Carter objected.

"You have been a stubborn man, Carter. But we can be equally stubborn," Hafi Amin said, his hand on the shoulder of his son. "We are the leaders and we will lead."

It was no use and Carter could see it. He was worried about

another detail. It was the morning of the battle and Marianne hadn't shown up.

As if he had read his mind, Haami asked about the new weapons they would use. "My men have spotted a caravan just a few miles to the northwest. They are heading for our camp. Are they carrying the new weapons?"

Carter raced to the highest rocky outcropping and pointed his glasses to the northwest. He saw the caravan of donkeys and the face of the bright young woman who rode with them.

EIGHTEEN

Major Alexei Rykov of the Spetsnaz sat on a rock and looked over his troops. He had given them a ten-minute rest period. Many were having a cigarette and boasting about the victory to come. They were ahead of schedule. They would rest there and start out again in the early afternoon.

"We could be in position early if we proceeded now," his second in command offered.

"We will move on my order," Rykov said tersely. This was the first sortie he'd been in for years that could end in bloodshed. He wasn't in a hurry to see the first of his men killed, as some surely would be. He lit a cigarette and leaned back against another boulder. "We have lots of time. Tell the men to relax," he commanded.

"But we should get to the rendezvous early and scout it thoroughly," the younger man persisted.

Rykov looked at the overeager officer with scorn. "Enough, Captain. "We've got plenty of time. I'll tell you when to move out."

Captain Vadim Munshin, commanding the KGB, trotted ahead of his column, sweat pouring from his chin. Like the

177

Spetsnaz, the KGB special guards were macho: they felt they had to trot everywhere. But Munshin did not always agree with KGB dogma or the stupidity of some of their practices. The thought plagued him as yard after yard passed beneath his tired feet. This was the height of idiocy. To dog trot in the mountains of Afghanistan was stupid. But all of the military was stupid. He cursed his back luck at having an influential relative in the Politburo who thought the KGB was the place for him. A foreign posting would have been nice. American women for a change, or French.

For all his complaining, and he kept it to himself, he was as fit as any man in his command. He would send them to meet the enemy with the apparent dedication of his superiors, but deep down his heart wasn't in it.

We don't need this, he thought. "Halt!" he yelled at the top of his lungs. He sat on a rocky shelf breathing hard, reaching for a cigarette. To hell with orders. They would march the rest of the way like ordinary mortals. He was tired of being a superman.

From his rocky perch miles away from the two Soviet groups. Carter had his glasses trained first left then right, searching for the pincer groups let by Haami and Amin senior. Marianne was at his side. She had created a sensation when she arrived. She'd had enough sense to keep her hands off Carter when her caravan pulled in, but the look she had given him was evident to everyone. He had given her the job of training the men who would handle the SAM launchers. When the timing was right, she would deploy the men for maximum effect.

Carter could see movement well to his left. Marianne had scrounged a half-frozen-walkie-talkies from the caravan's supplies, and Carter used his now. "I can see you, Haami. Keep your people right where they are."

"We will stay here, Mr. Carter?" Haami asked.

"Your position is perfect," he replied over the static. They were at maximum signal range. "Keep them quiet. We don't want any noise. A rifle scratched against rock can be heard for miles out here."

He panned to the far right. A force of a thousand ragtag *mujaheddin* were crouched in a rocky defile out of sight. The glasses were powerful and it was a clear day. He could see the smoke from their cigarettes.

He thumbed the button. "Hafi Amin. I can see your force. Come in," Carter said.

"I am here, Mr. Carter. Are we in the right place?"

"Perfect. Did you hear me talk to Haami?"

"Yes."

"Good. Keep your men quiet and tell them to put out their cigarettes. The enemy can smell the smoke when they get closer."

"How long, Mr. Carter?" Hafi Amin asked.

"A couple of hours. I can't see them yet. "I've got to talk with Salman. Over and out."

Carter spent a full half hour with Salman making sure he understood every phase of his part in the operation. "Your men are the key," he told the young Afghan. "They must get in, create the diversion that will spring the trap, and get out with as few casualties as possible."

"My men will die for our country's freedom if need be," the young leader said.

"They don't have to die," Carter reminded him. "Keep your walkie-talkie on so I can get to you when I have to. Keep your men quiet when they are in position, and no smoking. We want to see the enemy close to your position first. For now, let the men rest. They'll have to move fast when the time comes."

It was almost five o'clock, 1700 hours. The KGB would be taking up the west slope in less than an hour, Carter thought. If he'd had to issue the orders again, he'd have spread out the time. It would have been better for one to arrive well ahead than for them to come face-to-face, but it was too late for second thoughts.

At 1730 hours he saw the KGB group coming from the south. When they passed rocky outcroppings, he could see their camouflage uniforms. They were moving into position with caution.

He raised the glasses and looked further out. Another group was entering the valley from a rocky pass about five miles to the south. Their path was further to the southeast. They wouldn't pick up the tracks of the first group unless they had scouts ranging a couple of miles on either side, and Carter hadn't seen any.

The KGB group climbed down the defile at the bottom of the valley and came to their position on the west side. They formed up momentarily at the edge of the defile and then climbed to higher ground to take up their positions. It was 1745 hours.

Carter kept the glasses on the other group. He heard the rattle of small arms against rock behind him and literally flew toward Salman. "Get them all out of sight! No noise . . . none! And no smoking! They have to be invisible!"

He returned to his vigil. The Spetsnaz had come up the valley, keeping well to the east of the defile. They halted for final orders and took up positions well up the slope, about fifty yards away from the defile and a hundred yards from the other force. If they were aware of each other, they weren't showing signs of alarm.

The final curtain was about to go up. It was 1755 hours. Now that the two elite groups were in position, Carter reflected on the maneuvering that it had taken to get them that far. He chuckled to himself as he thought about the result.

Marianne stood a few paces behind him. "It's time to place your people," he said, turning to her. "Make sure each of your men is placed well away from the others. Have they got their firing sequence down?"

"I've done my job," she said. "Do you want me to do anything else?"

"When you get your men in position, stay with me and start using the video camera."

Carter spoke to Salman on the walkie-talkie. The Afghans moved out in single file. They were doing what they did best. The cover was just enough to make them invisible. The defile, a deep ditch cut through the valley by flash rains, was grown over by low brush that was sufficient to hide them completely.

It took fifteen minutes to get them to the valley floor and ready for the fight. Many of the men carried old M-16s, guns that would be almost useless except to make one hell of a racket. Fully a third of the men carried the new M-16A2s equipped with grenade launchers. They each wore a pouch of grenades hanging from their belts.

Salman carried an M-16A2 with a grenade down the pipe. He looked down the line at his men, all of whom were grinning with excitement, their white teeth shining from black beards streaked with dust. He looked at his watch. He didn't know Carter's whole plan, and the gaps didn't help his nerves. It was 1810 hours. He cocked the grenade launcher and pulled the trigger.

Salman's grenade, a fragmentation missile, landed twenty feet from Major Rykov. Razor-sharp pieces of steel blew the men near Rykov to shreds, and the major himself was hit. He could feel the numbness in his left thigh. His hand came away covered with blood.

"Fire!" he shouted. But his voice was lost in the roar that had started with the first blast. Grenades were exploding everywhere. His men were going down like trees in a hurricane.

Rykov ran up the slope to the end of his line to get a better view of his position. Grenades were exploding on both sides of the defile. His men were being cut to ribbons.

At the top of the hill, well above the fury below, the video camera recorded the battle through a wide-angle lens. Marianne felt her stomach lurch at the carnage, but she kept the camera rolling. She didn't want to show her fear. Carter stood close by. Apparently, everything was going as he'd planned. She heard him call in Haami and Amin to advance from the rear.

Salman gave the signal for his people to retreat. Their pouches were empty. Sixty of them had pumped seven grenades each up the hills, some to the left and some to the right. They had seen many Russians, the hated enemy, blown to bits.

The men without launchers had their M-16s on full auto, emptying the clips and slapping in new ones as fast as they knew how. Some had looked up to see Russian soldiers hit by their fire and screamed in victory, their faces gleaming in the half light, their revenge sweet.

Now they ran for cover at the order of their leader. To run was not their style, but their leaders had agreed. They crouched low, one after the other, and slipped through the overgrown defile to the safety of the heights above.

As they moved out, a hail of steel started to come their way from either side of the narrow ditch. Most of the firing was sporadic and ineffective. A few grenades exploded nearby, but the fragmentation spread over their heads. They could feel the concussion, however, and it knocked them down but few were wounded. The American had provided protection. So far everything he had planned had worked.

At the first explosion, Captain Vadim Munshin of the KGB was shocked to find his group in an ambush. How could his people in Moscow have been so wrong? He ran up the hill and beyond the field of fire. He had to see the whole battlefield. What he saw turned his blood to ice. A thousand screaming *mujaheddin* were at his back.

Lieutenant Stanislaw Mikoyan watched Munshin go. Men were falling all around him. A piece of steel struck him in the side and knocked him down. Slowly, holding on to a shattered tree stump, Mikoyan pulled himself up. He surveyed the scene. Someone below, hidden by the brush at the bottom of the hill, was lobbing grenades up the hill.

How had Munshin let them get trapped so badly? He slipped his field glasses from their case and trained them on the ditch. Afghans! They were dressed in Russian uniforms as he'd been told to expect. Damn the rebel bastards!

He could see the grim smiles on the faces of the enemy. He knew they had the initial advantage, but they were poorly positioned.

His glasses picked up the hopelessness of the Afghan position. *He had them!* They were trapped like rats. He held his torn side with one hand and shouted above the din for the other officers. He knew what they had to do. One fast attack down the hill would get them. And they would feel cold steel. He would order a bayonet charge.

First he'd saturate the ditch and the other side of the hill with mortars and grenades. Then he'd order a charge. His men would go in with their AK-47s on full auto and finish the job with steel blades. They'd get those bastards! No one was going to kill off the best damned outfit in the Soviet. No one stupid enough to fight from a ditch. They had signed their own death warrant.

He looked once again to see where Munshin had gone and saw the horde come at them from the rear. The scream of the Afghans' battle cry caught up with him at the same time.

Salman Amin found himself in the midst of the group scrambling to get back up the hill without being caught in a murderous cross fire. What the hell was taking so long? he wondered. The ones at the front seemed to be so damned slow.

He was out of the line of fire now. As the American had planned, the ditch was offering cover for small-arms fire, and the enemy hadn't recovered enough to saturate them with grenades or mortar fire.

Come on! His senses screamed for relief, for an advance to safety for them all. The men behind him would soon be catching hell if they didn't make better progress.

He stopped to let some of the others pass as he poked his head above the ditch. All the men he could see were dead Russians, sprawled in their own blood. All the firing was coming from higher on either side of the hill. It must be from his father's people and Haami's.

He looked up at their original position. The woman with the camera was a dot on the crest. Carter was beside her. They weren't taking cover, but the enemy was too preoccupied to see them.

Grenades were flying over his head now from one side of the ditch to the other. The noise was deafening. The battlefield smell of death hung in the air, filling the ditch.

He was further up the hill now and paused to look below. He could see a few of his men prone in the ditch. Some hobbled up the hill nursing wounds. The ones who were dead had taken rounds in the head. There was no way they could go back for them.

The sun as beginning to dip behind the peaks. The valley darkened quickly. He started up the hill again, stopping near the top to look down. Both sides were preparing for an all-out battle. He raised his glasses. The last of the daylight flashed from cold steel. He could see bayonets on some of the rifles.

"How many did you lose?" Carter asked him when he reached the top.

"Five. Maybe six," he answered.

"One is too many," Carter said. "But in a battle like the one you took them through, that's not bad. You did very well."

When Salman's men had passed, Carter took up a position at the edge of the ridge on his belly, his glasses trained on the scene below. He could see brown uniforms moving slowly toward the ditch, cautiously, looking for the source of the original firing.

Mortars started dropping in from farther up the hill to the opposite side. They were answered by the other group. Huge holes opened up on both sides, explosions, ear-splitting, tossing dirt and shrubs, cloth and flesh, spraying the advancing men with gory debris.

The enemy forces were divided, some firing at the defile, others trying to defend themselves from the attack from their rear.

The popping sound of small-caliber grenade launchers joined the roar of the mortars. The clatter of hundreds of Kalashnikovs emptying their banana-shaped clips filled the air. Flashes of light revealed men being torn to shreds, their guts spread among the living. The scene was a page from hell, seen in advance, a message to men who tempted fate.

Some of the Soviet foot soldiers reached the bottom of the hill. They saw patches of brown uniforms on the other side and charged. Screams of hate, frustration, and fear were torn from their throats as they plunged into the ditch, gutting their enemies, tearing at cloth and flesh with razor-sharp knives, adrenaline charging them, giving them strength they'd never had before, adding a will to kill that training had only guessed at, leading them to a red sea of torn bodies on both sides as the ditch churned with men who drew back rifles and plunged and plunged again at bodies already dead in the frenzy of killing and the will to survive.

Carter had seen enough. He pulled a stubby gun from his belt, broke open the breach, shoved in a shell, and snapped it closed.

It was almost dark in the valley. It was a psychedelic hellhole, alternately pitch-black at one moment and lit by the flash of a mortar or a grenade the next.

He raised the pistol and fired. The star shell burst over the valley, lighting the scene below. The battle was still in progress, ants tearing the flesh from ants. As the white light bathed the whole scene, men still stood, miraculously, as a steady roar of motors grew to overpower the sound of battle.

NINETEEN

They came over the hill like prehistoric flying monsters and hung there as if suspended, their rotors flashing in the waning light of the star shell.

Carter had heard of them, seen one or two on the ground, but he had never seen them in full battle array. They were awesome, stubby, all angles, and bristling with enough firepower to sink a battleship.

Six HI-24 gunboats started to circle, following their leader who took his brutal-looking machine in a slow turn. He had no fear of enemy aircraft. He had no concern for ground fire. He knew what he faced. Each of the ugly ships had two AA-8 air-to-ground missiles, four 60mm multicannon, and they carried wing pods that Carter didn't recognize.

Lazily, as if on a pleasure outing, the leader turned to face the mass of men below, sitting ducks in a barrel of blood.

Carter left Marianne to continue her chronicle of the battle and made his way to the SAM surface-to-air missile battery.

"Which of you is to shoot first?" He asked the first man he met.

The Afghan was a brute of a man. He held the SAM on his

shoulder as if it were a toy. "Ezah, the little man on the end."
He pointed to his right.

Carter found Ezah struggling with the SAM, too great a
weight for his slight frame. He was standing on a rocky ledge
near the top of the cliff. Carter steadied the tube, standing well
to one side, and shouted over the noise of the choppers. "Wait
until they are clear of our troops before you fire. We don't
want their wreckage to land on our people."

As he was shouting into the wind, the choppers, unaware of
the threat, whirled to their first attack. In the process they were
a mile away and clear of the troops on the ground. Carter let
go of the tube for a moment and fired another star shell. When
Carter held the tube again, the small man triggered his missile.
It left the launch tube in a flash of fire, scorching the rock wall
behind them. The repercussion hit Carter and Ezah in their
backs. The little man went headfirst from the ledge. Carter
caught his robe and pulled him back as the SAM launcher
clattered to the rocks below.

The two men, Afghan and American, sat back on the ledge,
shaken. Carter jumped up as an orange and red ball of fire
blossomed in the sky a couple of miles away. The debris of the
HI-24 fanned out, leaving contrails of smoke and fire as they
fell to the ground. The small Afghan jumped up and down on
the ledge, hugging Carter around the middle.

In the fading light of the star shell, the remaining HI-24s
whirled, hung suspended in the air, and faced the cliff. Carter
shook himself loose and raced around the corner of the cliff.
the choppers started an attack, slowly, aiming straight for the
SAM battery on the cliff.

Before he could shout orders, the number two SAM shot
from the launcher. The backlash toppled the shooter off the
cliff to the rocks below. The missile took off on a straight line
for the oncoming choppers, homed in on one, and blew it out
of the sky. This time the debris fell on the men that were
charging the Spetsnaz under the command of Hafi Amin.

Carter ran from man to man warning them against the
powerful recoil. The choppers stopped, hovered for a second

or two, and took off under full power. Nothing in the arsenals of the world threatened aircraft, particularly slow-flying aircraft, as much as a SAM. When the launchers were portable as these were, they were even more of a threat.

As the choppers wheeled away, the leader brought up the rear. He fired a random shot at the cliffside as he turned. The AA-8 air-to-ground missiled chewed a huge hole from the cliff and lit the scene in a bright yellow ball of flame. The two men Carter had just passed were vaporized, their remains blown from the rock face.

The surviving SAM launch men faced the ball of fire and watched the downward drift of rock chips and human remains with horror. As the HI-24s made smaller and smaller targets in the sky, the Afghans, the heavy tubes on their shoulders, fired a salvo that sent a half-dozen missiles rocketing in straight lines for the retreating choppers.

Carter was surrounded by smoke and rock dust. He heard explosions in the distance. By the time the smoke cleared, all he could see was the flaming remains of three or four choppers heading for the ground about five miles away. One of them might have escaped. If one did, they might expect an all-out advance from General Lorkh's forces. On the other hand, if all the chopper pilots had been in on Popolov's plot, what was the survivor going to tell Lorkh? Carter made a mental note to get the Afghan troops out of action as fast as possible.

He looked around when all the smoke had cleared. Four men sat against the rock face, their faces chalky white. Four survivors out of ten. Not a good count.

On the top of the cliff, Carter found Marianne putting the camera into a leather case. He looked out at the battlefield. The action had stopped. Afghan *mujaheddin*, like swarms of ants far below, waved their rifles in the air and danced up and down. The area around the defile was pockmarked, the brush torn up or burned. Whisps of smoke from grenade or mortar hits drifted off into the wind. The camouflaged bodies on the ground were still.

Salman Amin and Jalaludin Haami stood apart, hugging each other. Instead of cheers, they stood with tears running down their faces.

"Hafi is dead," Haami said as Carter walked up. "He led the charge against the Spetsnaz rear and caught the first of their fire."

"I'm sorry," Carter said. "He was a great leader. But we can't grieve for him now. It would be wise to clear the battlefield of your men. The Soviets could mount reprisals at any time. Get them all back to camp as fast as possible."

He turned and walked to Marianne. "Did you get it all?" he asked.

"Most of it. Enough to show all the formations," she said. "My God, the SAMs were spectacular."

"We lost more than half of our SAM men," he said, feeling that part of the blame fell on his shoulders. "And Hafi is dead," he added.

"I know. So it might all have been in vain."

"I don't think so. We'll know better tonight."

They sat around a campfire eight hours later. They were all sad and weary. Their women had fed them and they had their pipes filled and glowing nicely. Marianne sat with them, a concession to her part in the arms delivery and training.

"Hafi will be missed," Haami said. "We will bury him tomorrow."

Six of the elders of the camp sat around the fire with Carter, Marianne, Haami, and Salman. They had little to say. The day had given them a decisive battle, but they had lost many of their young men. The highlight had been the shooting down of the HI-24s. Soviet flying men would be more cautious in the future.

"Hafi will be missed," one of the old men repeated. "He died proud of his son. Salman proved himself today, more than ever before."

"I agree, and I have a suggestion," Carter said, taking his turn in the conversation. The flames lit their faces, dark and shadow, flickering light, drifting smoke. They were images from a dark and mysterious past. They were warriors of the past and present, leaders of the future. "The international community recognizes Jalaludin Haami as a strong leader. A man you all will follow. The loss of your beloved Hafi would weaken your image if his death were known to the enemy and others."

"What are you getting at?" Haami asked.

"Salman proved he is a courageous leader," Carter said. "And he looks like his father. He cannot completely replace Hafi in your hearts, but he can lead, and the rest of the world can be fooled."

"How?" one of the elders asked.

"Hafi Amin still lives. We don't tell the world that Hafi is dead. Let Salman grow his beard longer. Tint it with gray. In time, when your men are accustomed to Salman's leadership, Hafi can truly die."

Salman smiled across the fire at Carter. A strong bond had grown between them in the last twenty-four hours.

"I will be able to tell my leaders that the Afghan rebels fight on," Carter said. "I will tell them your leadership is strong and that we are friends and allies."

"Salman! Salman!" The chant rang out from the fire and echoed down the hill to the fires below where it was caught up by the men. The name echoed through the valley.

In the tents of the women, voices were raised, gentle voices, voices filled with emotion. They were the ones to mourn the dead, some to sleep alone. But they knew the ways of their men. They knew the name of their new leader. And they had lived through another day.

DON'T MISS THE NEXT NEW
NICK CARTER SPY THRILLER

COUNTDOWN TO ARMAGEDDON

The jukebox was turned down low. All the lights had been turned off except two dim bulbs behind the bar. It was almost one in the morning and the customers had long since been dispersed by Leduc. The Frenchman himself was somewhere out in the night.

Carter sat with the girl at a table in the center of the room, a bottle between them.

The taxi driver had returned at five minutes before midnight. What he had told Carter after slipping in through the rear door had been illuminating.

"There were two men, monsieur, not a man and a woman."

Carter had listened gravely to the driver's description of the two men, and then sent him on his way. Then he had huddled with Leduc.

"They won't use guns," Carter had said, "only as a last resort. And neither will I. If possible, I want to take one of them alive."

"Then use this," Leduc said, passing Carter the knife he had taken earlier in the bar fight.

Now they sat, waiting.

"They are not coming," the girl whispered, keeping up the pretense by running her hand up Carter's leg under the table.

"They'll come," Carter said, sliding one finger across her ample breast and kissing her lightly on the lips.

All at once the girl's eyes flickered away from him, over his shoulder, toward the hallway leading into the bar from the rear door. "He is here, the tall blond one."

Carter turned in his chair. "Lundesburg, what are you doing so far from the city?"

The man's eyes checked the room, under every table and behind the bar. When he was satisfied that there were just the three of them, he spoke. "I was drinking at another bar down the street. They told me there that I could find a good woman here. I saw you through the front window."

Carter laughed. "Sorry, old man, you're out of luck. I'm afraid the only woman in this place is mine for the night. But let me buy you a drink."

He nodded his head toward the bar. The girl stood. As she passed the big Swede, he grabbed her arm. In the same motion, he twisted her into him and put a knife to her throat.

"I'm not thirsty." He was calm, the eyes steady, not a quiver in the hand holding the knife. "Stand up and turn around, Carter."

"Carter? My name is—"

"Your name is Nick Carter. We sent a photograph to Moscow and got a reply at the consulate tonight. Sit there and don't move."

He shoved the girl into a chair, spun Carter around, and bent him over a table. With the blade at the back of Carter's neck, he skillfully ran his free hand all over the Killmaster's body.

"You're a brave man to travel the underbelly of Tangier without a weapon."

"Why would I need a weapon?" Carter said lightly.

The blow was sharp, across his shoulder. It was meant to be

painful, not disabling. Carter took it and maintained his position.

"Who else do you have on the ship?" the Swede hissed.

Carter decided to get to the point and do away with any further pretense. "I'll give you a chance to run, Lundesburg. Just give me Volga's identity."

The big Swede cursed and hit Carter again. The Killmaster rolled with this punch and hit the floor practically at the girl's feet.

"I could offer you the same thing in return for information," the Swede replied. "But you've just told me what I want to know."

Carter's eyes met the girl's. He nodded. Her hands grasped her skirt and pulled it to her waist. The long-bladed knife was along her inner thigh, held there by a garter.

Carter grasped the knife with one hand and shoved her chair back with the other. He didn't even try to withdraw the knife. He simply turned it, slitting the garter the same time he rolled.

The Swede's knife thudded into the wooden floor inches from Carter's shoulder.

The girl hit the floor and rolled, putting distance between herself and the two men.

Behind him, Carter heard the Swede curse and the sound of the knife being withdrawn. Then he was on his feet and turning.

Lundesburg was in a crouch, the knife up and ready. "You knew."

Carter nodded, giving the man an insolent grin. "I knew. I'm not going to kill you outright, Evor. I'm going to skin you, peel you until you start talking."

"You are a fool."

It began.

The Swede feinted, well, and his blade drove from Carter's gut. The Killmaster had already hooked a chair with his toe. He caught it with his free hand and jammed the back into the other man. It came up hard and high, catching Lundesburg under the chin, knocking him off-balance.

"Who is Volga, Lundesburg?"

"Believe it or not, Carter, I don't know. Not that it matters. . . ."

Then he was circling. Carter was moving with him, the two of them like poised panthers between the tables, each sizing up the other's stance and balance, strengths and weaknesses.

Then the Swede, with a snakelike hissing sound between his teeth, moved.

His hand was quick, daring like a striking viper. Carter caught the blade on his own, turning it aside and parrying. Lundesburg dodged, his body as agile as a bullfighter's, and the thrust was wide.

But it was almost the first score, and Carter saw beads of sweat pop out on the other man's face. And he saw something else: grudging respect in the other man's eyes.

The tall blond came again, this time in earnest, wanting it over with quickly. The blade arched at Carter's throat, then changed direction and plunged for his belly. The Killmaster stepped back nimbly and the slashing edge only got a portion of his shirt.

"Close, but no cigar, Lundesburg."

The frustrated Swede tried a backhand. Carter went under it with his blade up, and cut a ten-inch slash in the man's arm. The Swede roared, more in anger than pain, and recovered with another straightforward jab. This one caught another piece of Carter's shirt, but failed to find flesh.

The Swede finished the thrust off-balance. The Killmaster countered with double-armed slashes, shifting the blade from hand to hand each time. The result was one very bloody chest.

Lundesburg stepped back and looked down at himself in amazement.

"I told you," Carter growled, "I don't need to kill you. Let's talk."

The man looked up with pure hatred in his eyes. When the fresh attack came it wasn't at Carter; it was directed at the girl. The knife came up like lightning from the floor. If it would have struck, she would have been gutted like a fish.

But it didn't.

Again, Carter locked blades and got a grip on the other man's neck with his free hand. Their faces were close, so close that Carter could smell the other man's dinner on his breath.

And their eyes locked.

It was then that Carter knew it was useless. The man knew only one thing, kill or be killed. Compromise was not programmed into his brain.

Carter intentionally gave ground. The Swede's blade slipped loose and thrust at Carter's chest. The Killmaster twisted so it went between arm and body.

He felt the whisper of it as, once more, it slashed fabric. Then he wrenched his left hand away from Lundesburg's grappling left and with a smooth shifting motion threw the knife from right to left. His right went out and caught the Swede's knifehand, even as his left came over wielding the blade.

The change in hands, the change in balance, caught Lundesburg totally unprepared. Carter slit, quickly, expertly, and Lundesburg screamed. The knife dropped from his hand and blood poured down his chest from his severed throat.

He clawed at himself and gasped for air, air that had no conduit to his fevered lungs.

Carter stepped back, kicking the other man's across the room.

Lundesburg's eyes rolled up into his skull, came down again, and found Carter's. He was dying, his blood spurting through splayed fingers. He knew it, and the realization threw him into a panic.

He crashed over a few tables, his hands trying to stem the tide, and finally he sank to his knees. He stared at Carter for a long moment with eyes that were no longer fierce, only horrified.

Then he made an inarticulate gurgling sound in his throat and, wheeling, blood still spurting, he fell on his face.

The girl, calm through it all, stepped forward and leaned over him. Daintily, she pressed two fingers to the side of his throat and then rolled her eyes up at Carter.

"Mort, monsieur."

"Can you handle it?"

"Of course."

"Then do it. There's another one out there somewhere."

She nodded and Carter headed for the back door.

From COUNTDOWN TO ARMAGEDDON
A New Nick Carter Spy Thriller
From Jove in November 1988